Star of Wonder

Books by Daniel Mark Epstein

Poems
NO VACANCIES IN HELL
THE FOLLIES
YOUNG MEN'S GOLD
THE BOOK OF FORTUNE

Prose
THE HEATH GUIDE TO POETRY
THE HEATH GUIDE TO LITERATURE

Plays
JENNY AND THE PHOENIX
THE MIDNIGHT VISITOR

STAR OF WONDER

AMERICAN STORIES & MEMOIRS

Daniel Mark Epstein

The Overlook Press
Woodstock, New York

Star of Wonder

"Star of Wonder" first appeared in syndication in the following: the *Philadelphia Inquirer*, *The Baltimore Sun*, *The Cleveland Plain Dealer*, *Chicago*, *The Dayton News*, *The Portland Oregonian*, *Newsday*, *The Phoenix Republic*, *The Detroit News*, *The Los Angeles News*, *The Miami Herald*, *Suburbia Today*, *The Kansas City Star*, and *The St. Louis Post Dispatch*.

"The Case of Harry Houdini" first appeared in *The New Criterion*.

"The Great American Ghost" first appeared in syndication in *The Boston Globe*, *The St. Louis Post*, *The Toledo Blade*, *The Richmond Times*, *The Louisville Courier*, *The Cleveland Plain Dealer*, *The Dayton News*, and *The City Paper*, (Baltimore and Washington).

"The Star-Spangled Banner" appeared, in a slightly different form, under the title "America's #1 Song," in *The Atlantic Monthly*.

"The Violin Lesson" first appeared in *The National Review*.

"Passover Night and Easter Morning" first appeared in syndication in: *The Boston Globe*, *The Cleveland Plain Dealer*, *The Seattle Times*, *The San Jose Mercury*, *Suburbia Today*, and *The City Paper* (Baltimore and Washington).

Special thanks to Jack Beatty, William B. Eddins and Ande Zellman for their encouragement and editorial suggestions, and to Raymund Fitzsimons for his patience in answering my many questions about Harry Houdini.

First published in 1986 by
The Overlook Press
Lewis Hollow Road
Woodstock, New York 12498

Copyright © 1986 by Daniel Mark Epstein

Library of Congress Cataloging in Publication Date

Epstein, Daniel Mark.
Star of Wonder.

1. Epstein, Daniel Mark—Biography—Youth.
2. Poets, American—20th century—Biography—Youth.
I. Title.
PS3555.P65Z477   1986   811'.54 [B]   86-16301
ISBN 0-87951-257-1

Book design by The Sarabande Press

Printed in the U.S.A.

5 48 05143

To Wendy Roberts

*No testimony is sufficient to establish a miracle,
unless the testimony be of such a kind,
that its falsehood would be more miraculous,
than the fact, which it endeavors to establish.*
—David Hume

Contents

Star of Wonder

When my mother had taken me to see the skating bears and Santa's elves at work in the department store windows, and the giant pine tree on the mall with its spirals of colored lights, it would be time to leave the city. In those years I remember only as stories, my mother would return to her parents' home for Christmas. She would buckle me into my car seat and drive a hundred miles to the town of Vienna, Maryland, on the Eastern Shore.

The clapboard house smelled of cedar and sherry. It was brilliant with bayberry candles and holly and relatives and a huge upright piano with cracked ivories that knew only Christmas carols. My mother played while grandfather turned the pages of the Episcopal hymnbook. Everyone sang. I sat under the Christmas tree and recited "'Twas the night before Christmas. . ." from beginning to end, in a rage because no one would read it to me again. When everybody clapped, I ran and hid in a closet under the stairs.

The reason for this pilgrimage on Christmas is that mother had married a Jew. She appreciated his broad-mindedness but did not want to press it by decking his halls with the frills and bangles of her most clamorous holiday.

She need not have worried. Just before my sister was born, my mother's Hudson, chugging toward Vienna, rolled over in a snowbank. No one was hurt, but when my father heard about it on New Year's Day, he declared a blockade. All

Christmases henceforth, with all their rites and rituals, would be conducted under his roof. No tree would be too tall, no carol too sentimental, no bauble too gaudy. My father became Santa Claus, a role he played as if it had been written for him.

My father was as generous, but also as mysterious and mercurial, as the winking Saint Nick. He had wild black hair and stormy eyes and wore T-shirts and khaki trousers in all kinds of weather. My father was in the coin-machine business. He jingled with keys. He carried a pearl-handled revolver and enormous rolls of cash, and chain-smoked Lucky Strikes with such deftness that hardly anyone noticed. He disappeared for weeks at a time.

From his teens, my father had been the sole support of an extended family. He taught us to be mindful of our desires by giving us exactly what we needed 364 days a year, and then everything our hearts desired on Christmas day. I did not understand any of this then. I just tried to be good enough so Santa would bring me presents, and hoped my father would be there to watch me open them.

Chanukah came first, and then Christmas. Chanukah took longer, and the dates skipped around, and my father was a busy man. If there was any question about the propriety of celebrating both holidays, I was not aware of it. I went to Hebrew school, and my mother went to church, and sometimes I went with her. When I was seven, I got a tin menorah embossed with the Lion of Judah and the Crown of the Law. I taught my sister the *baruchas* as she worked her black curls into a tangle. We sang our blessings over the candles that flickered cheerfully on the breakfront across from the Christmas tree. Chanukah came first, celebrating a miracle in the past. Christmas was a miracle to come. The blessings of

Chanukah were certain and recited day after day; less certain were the blessings of Christmas. For there was always the mystery: "Do you think he'll come?"

My sister and I were always afraid that Santa might not come. I think it had something to do with our being Jewish. After all, Santa Claus had plenty of Christian children on his amazing itinerary without stopping to fill the stocking of a Jewish boy and his sister, no matter *how* good they had been all year.

Then there was the cautionary tale of Uncle Donald. My mother's uncle had not been all that a little boy was supposed to be in those innocent green years of the twentieth century. He had not said his prayers or minded his elders, eaten his parsnips or kept his room clean. Besides all those sins of omission it was hinted that Uncle Donald had *done* something, a thing so appalling and unkind that no one ever spoke of it again. We lay awake nights thrilling each other with the possibilities.

Whatever the case, Uncle Donald had not been good that year, and his record was on file with Santa Claus. Christmas morning, he bounded down the stairs. His long red stocking, which had hung on the chimneypiece with his brothers' and sisters' the night before, had vanished from its place under the brass pendulum of the Regulator clock. His stocking had been nailed in a distant corner. Poking from the hem was a brace of hickory switches. And under his stocking where he looked for presents, there were cakes of gleaming, spiteful coal.

So my sister and I were at great pains to be good, especially during the weeks before Christmas. Suspecting that my mother was an agent of Santa Claus (after all, she delivered our lists), we tried very hard to please her. And in December this mostly had to do with getting ready for Christmas.

There was a great deal to be done. My mother had a clear and exquisite vision of Christmas that she defended like a city in a state of siege. I would say it was like a turreted, gabled townhouse with lace curtains, all candlelit against the blizzard on a Victorian greeting card, but that would not do it justice. Her vision was not still; it was alive and fleeting, as all beautiful things must be. It was more like those winter scenes whose air is water, those tiny tableaus preserved under crystal domes a child can hold in his hand.

There is a thatched cottage with triangular pines on either side, and a girl in the doorway watching a couple in a horse-drawn sleigh. It all looks dead before you pick it up. But then you give it a shake and suddenly that frozen world awakens to time in the swirl and glitter of falling snow. The pines nod in the wind, and the windows shine. Light catches the eye of the waving girl as the lovers ride off, and muscles ripple under the horse's mane as he drinks the air. Then the sky clears, the last flake falls to rest and the glass world returns quietly to its watchful death.

It might snow, and it might not, but my mother was not relying upon heaven to provide the holiday atmosphere. There was a great deal to be done, and she was something of a storm herself. The house had to be cleaned from attic to basement in preparation for the chaos that comes with sudden wealth. Hair tied back beneath a paisley kerchief, mop in hand, she charged the barbarous clutter.

Then there was the moving. The Christmas tree would be raised in the dining room, where the banquet table, solid cherry, now stood. It was no great obstacle. I think that when we first came to the house, it had taken only four ex-marines to lift it. The real problem was the breakfront looming upon the opposite wall, where my mother wanted the table. She liked to view the breakfront through the archway that opened upon the living room. The breakfront weighed fifteen hundred pounds, more or less, and I think that the movers had removed a section of the roof and used a crane to install it. With my father away, I was the man in the house. Mother was very proud of my strength.

When we had finished rearranging the furniture, I lay panting on the couch, certain that Santa Claus must be touched by my devotion. I have heard there is some mystery about the construction of the Great Pyramid of Cheops, having to do with the hugeness of the building stones and the unfeasibility of transporting them miles into the desert. I have the answer. It was accomplished by an army of small boys desirous of pleasing their mothers.

At last it was time to bring in the tree. For several days it had lain in the stairwell under the back porch, its lopped trunk soaking in a kettle, nursing its wounded pride like a ransomed queen. It had been chosen from thousands for its shape and stature, its color and personality. If there were a dozen Christmas-tree concessions within driving distance, we were not satisfied until we had ransacked them all. Gloved attendants, recalling my mother from the year before, fled at our approach, hiding among the blue spruce trees or the Scotch pines they knew were beneath her consideration.

It would have to be a long-needle pine, the height of her raised hand, deep green with golden overtones at such and such a distance, feathery soft and so thick you could not see daylight through the branches. It must look lathe-turned for symmetry, and yet not so perfect that a casual admirer might mistake it for man-made. It must be, in short, such a tree as

God might have made upon my mother's instructions. I have not seen such a tree in years, and I wonder if they still make them.

But when I was a boy, there was one tree like that every year, and we would not stop looking until we found it. One year, the search kept me from going skating with Sammy Goldstein. "You have to do what?" he cried, amazed. "What kind of a *goyisha* business is *that*?" I think he was envious of my Christmases, though he did not have the slightest idea of what they were all about.

My father was far away, and we waited for him to call. The aromas of port wine and black currants filled the house as his favorite fruitcake baked in the oven. Nat King Cole was singing "Chestnuts roasting on an open fire. . . ," his baritone crooning from the grooves of a seventy-eight recording so crosshatched from Christmases that it snapped and crackled like a real fire. In honor and glory, we raised and anchored the tree.

The tree looked so splendid in the altogether, we could rest awhile before dressing it up. Cartons of regalia had been hauled up from the darkness near the water heater, where the ornaments had been mustering their brilliance. Wadded in tissues and packed in newspaper, one by one the ornaments sprang to light. Delicate as soap bubbles, frail as eggshells from ethereal hens, each bulb seemed an inheritance in itself, a miracle of survival, as if spared destruction for its beauty alone. My father had found them somewhere. There were perfect spheres in gold and pastel shades, with a mirror surface that, held close, would swell your forehead like Edgar Allan Poe's or your cheeks like Charles Laughton's. There were ovals designed with arabesques and tracery like Fabergé, or painted with ivied castles and manger scenes.

There was a glass raspberry that had to be hung high so no baby would eat it, and an emerald-colored bird of paradise with real tail feathers. My sister and I would quarrel over the bird, but I would let her hang it, because it was my job to hang the star.

The star looked more like a bishop's miter, until the light would fall into its concave silver face and burst into a halo at the treetop. After the electric lights and the tinsel and the bulbs had been hung, I would balance on the top rung of a wobbling ladder and crown the tree, and the three of us would cheer. There was the star of wonder. As the eternal light of wisdom and the constant light of hope, it was not only the holy star of Bethlehem, it must be the star of David as well.

The sun had set. The great star beamed upon the tin menorah that held court over the mountainous breakfront. It beamed upon the black yarmulke and the open prayerbook with its pages spattered with crimson wax. There were nine candles left in the box, for it was the last night of Chanukah. I rolled the spiral candles in my hands and considered which one should be the *shammash*. One was taller than the rest and looked destined for leadership, but I chose another that had suffered, a cracked candle that stood strong by force of determination and a sturdy wick. The other candles I twisted into their sconces. I scratched a stove match to life and lit the *shammash*, whose eager wick flamed up as if the fire were pulled from above.

The *shammash* would light the others, and then rest in an elevated sconce as we sang in praise of the king of the universe, who had commanded us to kindle the lights, and "who wrought miracles for our fathers, in days of old, at this season."

So there were two stories to be told in our house, in the heart of December when the yule logs crackled in our tiny fireplace, and wind stirred the brass bells tied with ribbons to the door. We prayed for snow that threatened more than it fell. Two stories, like the two stars of the season that were really one.

The first story was mine to tell because I knew it best. It was the story of Judah Maccabee with his name like a hammer, the Lion of Judah. He had arms like a prizefighter. Judah Maccabee was just as calm marching into battle as climbing the boughs of a laurel from which he spied the bloodthirsty Syrians. Their army numbered as the grains of sand upon the Jordan. The wicked King Antiochus had sent them. Antiochus had stolen the temple treasures and raised a pagan altar, and made women and children bow down. Judah Maccabee would fix *him*!

With his minyan of bearded warriors, Judah Maccabee swept down from the hills of Modin. His men were brave philosophers, so holy they could fight even on the sabbath. Swords in one hand, prayer books in the other, fighting and praying, they charged the pagans and scattered them, regaining the temple for Israel. There was great rejoicing. Judah rescued a battered menorah from beneath the hooves of some swine. But there was not enough oil to burn more than a few hours. "Thank God for small favors," said Judah Maccabee, and he lit the fire. It burned for eight days and eight nights.

The other story was told by my sister, with some prompting from my mother. My sister especially loved the Christmas story because of the animals, which she played with by the hour in the miniature crèche under the tree.

"Once upon a time," my sister began, "there was a baby. This baby was *so* special that a flock of magicians came thousands of miles on camels just to look at Him. A huge star had told them where He was. Jesus slept with the lambs and cows and chickens. His mother was very proud, and the animals all loved Him. The magicians said the baby was going to be king of the Jews.

"Now the wicked King Herod, who was Jewish, got very angry. He was going to kill all of the babies in Bethlehem!" My sister's eyes widened. "But then, an angel came to Joseph in a dream and told on Herod. And Joseph and Mary and Jesus ran away into Egypt, and Herod never did get them."

My mother explained that the child king was a promise of loving mercy and joy for humankind in a cruel time.

I suppose I was not the first Jewish boy to wonder what Judah Maccabee would have thought of King Herod. But as my mother's voice trailed away at the story's end, and the last embers glowed on the dark hearth, I was terribly ashamed of Herod, and as happy as anyone that the little boy had gotten away safely in His mother's arms.

My sister was nodding on my mother's shoulder as we heard a sound at the door that turned out to be the wind and some carolers down the street singing "Greensleeves." If my mother ever worried about my father, she never let us know it.

I could tell from her forehead that she was thinking hard about something, and I knew that it was a secret, maybe something she was wishing Santa would bring her. And I made a silent wish that she should have it, even if it cost me my bicycle.

It was time for bed.

"Do you think he'll come, Mama?" my sister murmured, half asleep.

My mother passed the question along to me.

"Do *you* think he'll come?"

My life passed before me. "I think he will," I said. And I hurried off to bed, because Santa Claus was never known to come to children who were awake, Jewish or Christian. My mother hugged me and heard my prayers as if this were no different than any other night. But there was no other night like this.

Through the casement window I watched the starry heavens for a sign. There were no satellites in those days to confuse the stargazer, and I searched for a moving constellation led by the red light of Rudolph's nose, hoping to glimpse the reindeer and sleigh as they glided onto our rooftop. I had a wonderful dream.

Mary and Joseph and Jesus are riding in the back seat of an open sleigh, against a waterfall of presents. Santa cracks his whip over the heads of the grinning reindeer. They are nearing the Egyptian border, a black line across the sands. "Faster!" cries Santa Claus, cracking his whip, when out of a palm tree leaps a highwayman with a dagger in his teeth, grabs Blitzen by the harness and drags the team to a halt.

They are surrounded by leering assassins on camels. Up trots Herod, twirling his mustache. "Let Mommy and Daddy go," he growls. "I want the boy. Give me the boy. . ." Mary holds Him tighter, and Joseph rises in protest. Then, out of the desert comes a thunder of hooves and a cloud of dust. It's. . . Judah Maccabee, leading his cavalry of bearded soldiers with flashing swords and black prayer books. Fighting and praying and praying and fighting, they scatter the cowardly villains. They hang Herod upside down from the palm tree, tip their yarmulkes and ride off into the sunset.

"Who was that?" asks Joseph, as they cross the border.

Santa Claus, who is the only one old enough to remember

him, smiles an admiring smile. "*That* was the Lion of Judah."

At daybreak, we were awakened by the sound of Bing Crosby singing "White Christmas" over the bonfire static of the archaic seventy-eight. I leapt out of bed, ran down the hall and into the dining room. The engine of an electric train flashed around the bend from behind the Christmas tree, through mountains of packages with flowery ribbons and bows. A clumsily wrapped bicycle showed its spokes in the chimney corner where our stockings were full to bursting. My mother and father were dancing in the living room.

"Ho, ho, ho!" called my father, rubbing the sand from his eyes, and I could see he had not slept in a long time.

The Case of
Harry Houdini

When my grandfather was a boy he saw Houdini, the wildhaired magician, escape from a riveted boiler. He would remember that image as long as he lived, and how Harry Houdini né Ehrich Weiss the rabbi's son, defeated the German Imperial Police at the beginning of the twentieth century. Hearing those tales and others even more incredible, sixty years after the magician's death we cannot help but wonder: What did the historical Houdini *really* do? And how on earth did he do it?

The newspaper accounts are voluminous, and consistent. The mere cataloguing of Houdini's escapes soon grows tedious, which they were not, to be sure, in the flesh. But quickly: the police stripped him naked and searched him thoroughly before binding his wrists and ankles with five pairs of irons. Then they would slam him into a cell and turn the key of a three-bond burglarproof lock. He escaped, hundreds of times, from the most secure prisons in the world. He hung upside down in a straightjacket from the tallest buildings in America, and escaped in full view of the populace. He was chained hand and foot and nailed into a packing case weighted with lead; the packing case was dropped from a tugboat into New York's East River and ninety seconds later Houdini surfaced. The packing case was hauled up intact, with the manacles inside, still fastened. He was sealed into a paper bag and got out without disturbing the seal. He was sewn into a huge football, into the belly of a whale, and escaped. In California he was buried six feet underground, and clawed his way out. He did this; he did that. These are facts that cannot be exaggerated, for they were conceived as exaggerations. We know Houdini did these things because his actions were more public than the proceedings of Congress, and most of them he performed over and over, so no one would miss the point.

How did he do such things? For all rational people who are curious, sixty years after the magician's death, there is good news and bad news. The good news is that we know how the vast majority of Houdini's tricks were done, and the explanations are as fascinating as the mystery was. Much of our knowledge comes from the magician's writings, for Houdini kept ahead of his imitators by exposing his castoff tricks. We have additional information from technicians and theater historians. Magicians will not reveal Houdini's secrets—their code forbids it. But so much controversy has arisen concerning his powers, so much conjecture they may have been supernatural, extraordinary measures have been taken to assure us Houdini was a *mortal* genius. Many secrets have leaked out, and others have been discovered by examining the props. So at last we know more about Houdini's technique than any other magician's.

The disturbing news is that, sixty years after Houdini's last performance, some of his more spectacular escapes remain unexplained. And while magicians, such as the excellent Doug Henning, are bound not to expose their colleagues, they are free to admit what mystifies them. They know how Houdini walked through the brick wall at Hammerstein's Roof Garden, in 1914, but they do not know how he made the elephant disappear in 1918. This trick he performed only for a few months in New York. And when people asked him why he did not continue he told them that Teddy Roosevelt, a great hunter, had begged him to stop before he exhausted the world's supply of pachyderms.

But before we grapple with the mysteries, let us begin with what we can understand. Let us begin with my grandfather's favorite story, the case of Harry Houdini versus the German police. Houdini's first tour of Europe depended upon the good will and cooperation of the law. When he arrived in London in 1900 the twenty-six-year-old magician did not have a single booking. His news clippings eventually inspired an English agent who had Houdini manacled to a pillar in Scotland Yard. Seeing that Houdini was securely fastened, Superintendent Melville of the Criminal Investigation Department said he would return in a couple of hours, when the escapist had worn himself out. By the time Melville got to the door the magician was free to open it for him.

The publicity surrounding his escape from the most prestigious police force in the world opened up many another door for the young magician. Booked at the Alhambra theater in London he performed his "challenge" handcuff act, which had made him famous on the vaudeville circuit. After some card tricks and standard illusions, Houdini would stand before the proscenium and challenge the world to restrain him with ropes, straitjackets, handcuffs, whatever they could bring on, from lock shops, prisons and museums. A single failure might have ruined him. There is no evidence that he ever failed, though in several cases he nearly died from the effort required by sadistic shackles. The "challenge" act filled the Alhambra theater for two months. Houdini might have stayed there if Germany had not already booked him; the Germans could hardly wait to get a look at Houdini.

As he had done in America and England, Houdini began his tour of Germany with a visit to police headquarters. The Dresden officers were not enthusiastic, yet they could hardly refuse the magician's public invitation to lock him up. A refusal would suggest a crisis of confidence; and like their colleagues the world over, the Dresden police viewed Houdini's news clippings as so much paper in the balance against their locks and chains. Of course the Dresden police had no more success than those of Kansas City, or San Francisco, or Scotland Yard. Their manacles were paper to him. The police chief reluctantly signed the certificate Houdini demanded, but the newspapers gave him little coverage.

So on his opening night at Dresden's Central Theater, Houdini arranged to be fettered in the leg irons and manacles of the Mathildegasse Prison. Some of the locks weighed forty pounds. The audience, packed to the walls, went wild over his escape, and the fact he spoke their language endeared him further. If anything could have held him captive it would have been the adoring burghers of Dresden, who mobbed the theater for weeks. The manager wanted to buy out Houdini's contract with the Wintergarten of Berlin, so as to hold him over in Dresden, but the people of Berlin could not wait to see the magician.

Houdini arrived in Berlin in October of 1900. The first thing he did was march into the police station, strip stark naked and challenge the jailors. They could not hold him. This time Count von Windheim, the highest-ranking policeman in Germany, signed the certificate of Houdini's escape. The Wintergarten was overrun. The management appealed to the theater of Houdini's next engagement, in Vienna, so they might hold him over an extra month in Berlin. The Viennese finally yielded, demanding an indemnity equal to Houdini's salary for one month. When the magician, at long last, opened at the Olympic Theater in Paris, December of 1901, he was the highest paid foreign entertainer in French history.

But meanwhile there was big trouble brewing in Germany. It seems the police there had little sense of humor about this Jew's peculiar gifts, and Houdini quickly exhausted what little patience they had. In Dortmund he escaped from the irons that had bound Glowisky, a notorious murderer beheaded three days before. At Hanover the police chief, Count von Schwerin, plotted to disgrace Houdini, challenging him to escape from a special straitjacket reinforced with thick leather. Houdini agonized for one and a half hours while von Schwerin looked on, his jubilant smile melting in wonder, then rage, as the magician worked himself free.

The cumulative anger of the German police went public in July of 1901. Inspector Werner Graff witnessed Houdini's escape from all manacles at the Cologne police station, and vowed to end the humiliation. It was not a simple matter of pride. Graff, along with von Schwerin and other officials, feared Houdini was weakening their authority and inviting jailbreaks, if not other kinds of antisocial behavior. So Graff wrote a letter to Cologne's newspaper, the *Rheinische Zeitung*. The letter stated that Houdini had escaped from simple restraints at the police headquarters by trickery; but his publicity boasted he could escape from restraints *of any kind*. Such a claim, Graff wrote, was a lie, and Houdini ought to be prosecuted for fraud.

Though he knew the letter was nonsense the magician could not ignore it, for it was dangerous nonsense. If the police began calling him a fraud in every town he visited, Houdini would lose his audience. So he demanded that Graff apologize and the newspaper publish a retraction. Graff refused, and other German dailies reprinted his letter. Should Harry Houdini sue the German policeman for libel? Consider the circumstances. Germany, even in 1901, was one of the most authoritarian states in the world. Houdini was an American, a Jew who embarrassed the police. A libel case against Graff would turn upon the magician's claim he could escape from *any* restraint, and the courtroom would become an international theater. There a German judge and jury would try his skill, and should they find it wanting, Houdini would be washed up, exiled to play beer halls and dime museums. Only an artist with colossal pride and total confidence in his methods would act as Houdini did. He hired the most prominent trial lawyer in Cologne, and ordered him to sue Werner Graff and the Imperial Police of Germany for criminal libel.

There was standing room only in the Cologne *Schöffengericht*. The judge allowed Werner Graff to seek out the most stubborn locks and chains he could find, and tangle Houdini in them, in full view of everyone. Here was a hitch, for Houdini did not wish to show the crowd his technique. He asked the judge to clear the courtroom, and in the ensuing turmoil the magician released himself so quickly no one knew how he had done it. The *Schöffengericht* fined the astonished policeman and ordered a public apology. So Graff's lawyer appealed the case.

Two months later Graff was better prepared. In the *Strafkammer*, or court of appeals, he presented thirty letters from legal authorities declaring that the escape artist could not justify his advertisements. And Graff had a shiny new pair of handcuffs. The premier locksmith of Germany had engineered the cuffs especially for the occasion. Werner Graff explained to the judge that the lock, once closed, could never be opened, even with its own key. Let Houdini try to get out of these.

This time the court permitted Houdini to work in privacy, and a guard led the magician to an adjacent chamber. Everyone else settled down for a long wait, in a chatter of anticipation. They were interrupted four minutes later by the entrance of Houdini, who tossed the manacles on the judge's bench. So the *Strafkammer* upheld the lower court's decision, as did the *Oberlandesgericht* in a "paper" appeal. The court fined Werner Graff thirty marks and ordered him to pay for the trials as well as a published apology. Houdini's next poster showed him in evening dress, his hands manacled, standing before the judge, jurors and a battery of mustachioed policemen. Looking down on the scene was a bust of the Kaiser against a crimson background, and a scroll that read: "The Imperial Police of Cologne slandered Harry Houdini . . .were compelled to advertise 'An Honorary Apology' and pay costs of the trials. By command of Kaiser Wilhelm II, Emperor of Germany."

Now this is surely an extravagant tale, and it will seem no less wonderful when we understand the technique that made it come true. When Houdini took on the Imperial Police in 1901, he was not whistling in the dark. By the time he left America at the end of the nineteenth century he had dissected every kind of lock he could find in the new world, and whatever he could import from the old one. Arriving in London, Houdini could write that there were only a few kinds of British handcuffs, "seven or eight at the utmost," and these were some of the simplest he had ever seen. He searched the markets, antique shops and locksmiths, buying up all the European locks he could find so he could dismantle and study them.

Then during his Berlin engagement he worked up to ten hours a day at Mueller's locksmith on the Mittelstrasse, studying restraints. He was the Bobby Fischer of locks. With a chessmaster's foresight Houdini devised a set of picks to release every lock in existence, as well as *any he could imagine*. Such tireless ingenuity produced the incandescent light bulb and the atom bomb. Houdini's theater made a comparable impact on the human spirit. He had a message which he delivered so forcefully it goes without mentioning in theater courses: Humankind cannot be held in chains. The European middle class had reached an impressionable age, and the meaning of Houdini's theater was not lost upon them. Nor was he mistaken by the aristocracy, who stayed away in droves. The spectacle of an American Jew bursting from chains by dint of ingenuity did not amuse the rich. They desperately wanted to demythologize him.

It was not about to happen in the German courtroom. When Werner Graff snapped the "new" handcuffs on Houdini, they were not strange to the magician. He had already invented them, so to speak, as well as the pick to open them, and the pick was in his pocket. Only a locksmith whose knowledge surpassed Houdini's could stop him; diligent study assured him that, as of 1901, there could be no such locksmith.

What else can we understand about the methods of Harry Houdini, né Ehrich Weiss? We know he was a superbly conditioned athlete who did not smoke or take a drop of alcohol. His straitjacket escapes he performed in full view of the world so that everyone could see he freed himself by main force and flexibility. He may or may not have been able to dislocate his shoulders at will—he said he could, and it seems no more marvelous than other skills he demonstrated. Friends reported that his toes could untie knots most of us could not manage with our fingers. And routinely the magician would hold his breath for as long as four minutes to work underwater escapes. To cheapen the supernatural claims of the fakir Rahman Bey, Houdini remained under water in an iron box for ninety minutes, as against the Egyptian's sixty. Examining Houdini, a physician testified that the fifty-year-old wizard had halved his blood pressure while doubling his pulse. Of course, more wonderful than any of these capabilities was the courage allowing him to employ them, in predicaments where any normal person would panic.

These things are known about Houdini. The same tireless ingenuity when applied to locks and jails, packing cases and riveted boilers—the same athletic prowess when applied at the bottom of the East River, or while dangling from a rope attached to the cornice of the Sun Building in Baltimore— these talents account for the vast majority of Houdini's exploits. As we have mentioned, theater historians, notably Raymund Fitzsimons in his *Death and the Magician*, have carefully exposed Houdini's ingenuity, knowing that nothing can tarnish the miracle of the man's existence. Their accounts are technical and we need not dwell on them, except to say they *mostly* support Houdini's oath that his effects were achieved by natural or mechanical means. The Houdini problem arises from certain outrageous effects no one has ever been able to explain, though capable technicians have been trying for more than sixty years.

Let us briefly recall those effects. We have mentioned the disappearing elephant. On January 7, 1918, Houdini had a ten-thousand-pound elephant led onto the bright stage of the Hippodrome in New York City. A trainer marched the elephant around a cabinet large enough for an elephant, proving there was space behind. There was no trapdoor in the floor of the Hippodrome, and the elephant could not fly. Houdini ushered the pachyderm into the cabinet and closed the curtains. Then he opened them, and where the elephant had stood there was nothing but empty space. Houdini went on with his program, which might have been making the Hippodrome disappear, for all the audience knew. A reporter for the *Brooklyn Eagle* noted: "The program says that the elephant vanished into thin air. The trick is performed fifteen feet from the backdrop and the cabinet is slightly elevated. That explanation is as good as any." After Houdini stopped making elephants disappear, nineteen weeks later, the trick would never be precisely duplicated.

That is the single "conventional" illusion of Houdini's repertoire that remains unexplained. He was not the greatest illusionist of his time, though he was among them. His expertise was the escape act, that specialty of magic furthest removed from theater, for its challenges are quite real and sometimes beyond the magician's control. It was the escapes, as his wife later wrote, that were truly dangerous, and Houdini privately admitted some anxieties about them. Give a wizard twenty years to build a cabinet which snuffs an elephant, and you will applaud his cleverness if he succeeds, in the controlled environment of his theater. But surrender the same man, stark naked, to the Russian police, who stake their honor upon detaining him in a convict van, and you may well suspect the intercession of angels should he get out.

And that is exactly what Houdini did, in one of the strangest and most celebrated escapes of his career. Strange, because it was Houdini's habit to escape only from barred jail cells where the locks were within easy reach, and only then after inspection, so he might hide picks in crannies, or excuse himself if he foresaw failure. But the Siberian Transport Cell made his blood boil. On May 11 of 1903 the chief of the Russian secret police searched the naked Houdini inside and out. The revolt of 1905 was in its planning stages and the Imperial Police were understandably touchy. The magician's wrists were padlocked and his ankles fettered before the police locked him into the *carette*. Mounted on a wagon, the zinc-lined steel cell stood in the prison courtyard in view of Chief Lebedoeff, his staff and a number of civilians. Twenty-eight minutes later Houdini was walking around the courtyard, stretching. Nobody saw him get out, but he was out. The police ran to the door of the *carette*. The door was still locked and the shackles lay on the floor of the undamaged van. The police were so furious they would not sign the certificate of escape, but so many people had witnessed the event that the news was soon being shouted all over Moscow. Doug Henning has written: "It remains one of his escapes about which the real method is pure conjecture."

In the Houdini Museum at Niagara Falls, Canada, you may view the famous *Mirror* handcuffs. If you are a scholar you can inspect them. In March of 1904 the London *Daily Mirror* discovered a blacksmith who had been working for five years to build a set of handcuffs no mortal man could pick. Examining the cuffs, the best locksmiths in London agreed they had never seen such an ingenious mechanism. The newspaper challenged Houdini to escape from them. On March 17, before a house of four thousand in the London Hippodrome, a journalist fastened the cuffs on Houdini's wrists and turned the key six times. The magician retired to his cabinet onstage, and the band struck up a march. He did not emerge for twenty minutes. Then he came out to hold the lock up to the light. Remember that most "challenge" handcuffs were regulation, and familiar to Houdini. He studied the lock in the light, and then went back into the cabinet, as the band played a waltz.

Ten minutes later Houdini stuck his head out, asking if he could have a cushion to kneel on. He was denied. After almost an hour Houdini stepped out of the cabinet again, obviously worn out, and his audience groaned. He wanted the handcuffs to be unlocked for a moment so he could take off his coat, as he was sweating profusely. The journalist denied the request, since Houdini had never before seen the handcuffs unlocked, and that might give him an advantage. Whereupon Houdini, in full view of four thousand, extracted a pen-knife from his pocket and opened it with his teeth. Turning the coat inside out over his head, he shredded it loose with the pen-knife, and returned to the cabinet. Someone called out that Houdini had been handcuffed for more than an hour. As the band played on, the journalists of the London *Daily Mirror* could taste the greatest scoop of the twentieth century. But ten minutes later there was a cry from the cabinet and Houdini leapt out of it, free, waving the handcuffs high in the air. While the crowd roared, several men from the audience carried Houdini, crying as if his heart would break, on their shoulders around the theater.

For all his other talents Houdini was a notoriously wooden actor, and we may assume the rare tears were altogether real, the product of an uncounterfeitable emotion. It is as if the man himself had been overwhelmed by his escape. Eighty years of technological progress have shed no light upon it. We know how Houdini got out of other handcuffs, but not these. As far as anyone can tell the *Mirror* handcuffs remain as the blacksmith described them — a set of handcuffs no mortal man could pick. One is tempted to dismiss the whole affair as mass hypnosis.

In the same Canadian museum you may view the Chinese Water Torture Cell, in which the magician hung upside down, in water, his ankles padlocked to the riveted roof. His escape from this cell was the crowning achievement of his stage career, and, though he performed it on tour the last ten years of his life, no one has the slightest notion how he did it. The gifted Doug Henning revived the act in 1975, on television. But he would be the first to tell you his was *not* Houdini's version, but his own, and he would not do it onstage before a live audience seven nights a week, with matinees on Wednesday and Saturday, because the trick would be unspeakably dangerous even if he could perform it there. When Houdini died he willed the contraption to his brother Hardeen, a fine magician in his own right. But Hardeen would not get in it either, and the instructions were to be burned upon his death. Again, as with the vanishing elephant, we are reviewing a stage illusion under controlled conditions, and may bow to a master's technical superiority, without fretting that he has used supernatural powers.

But the *Mirror* handcuffs and the Siberian Van Escape are troublesome, as are certain of Houdini's escapes from reinforced straitjackets, and packing cases underwater. So is the fact he was buried six feet underground, and clawed his way out. He only tried it once, and nearly died in the struggle, but the feat was attested, and you do not need a degree in physics to know it is as preposterous as rising from the dead. The weight of the earth is so crushing you could not lift it in the open air. Try doing this with no oxygen. The maestro himself misjudged the weight, and realizing his folly, tried to signal his crew when the grave was not yet full. They could not hear him and kept right on shoveling as fast as they could, so as not to keep him waiting. Then they stood back, to watch. A while later they saw his bleeding hands appear above the ground.

If we find Houdini's record unsettling, imagine what our grandparents must have thought of him. They knew almost nothing of his technique. Where we remain troubled by a few of his illusions and escapes, our ancestors were horrified by most of them. The European journalists thought he was some kind of hobgoblin, a shape shifter who could crawl through keyholes, or dematerialize and reappear at will. One can hardly blame them. Despite his constant reassurances that his effects were technical, and natural, the practical-minded layman could not believe it, and even fellow magicians were disturbed by his behavior.

So we come to the central issue in the case of Harry Houdini. It is an issue he carefully avoided in public, while studying it diligently in private. To wit: Can a magician, by the ultimate perfection of a technique, generate a force which, at critical moments, will achieve a supernatural result? Houdini's writings show this was the abiding concern of his intellectual life. It is, of course, the essential mystery of classical magic since before the Babylonians. Yet it remained a private and professional concern until Houdini's career forced it upon the public.

With the same determination that opened the world's locks, Houdini searched for an answer. His own technique was so highly evolved that its practice might have satisfied him, but his curiosity was unquenchable. He amassed the world's largest collection of books pertaining to magic and the occult, and no less a scholar than Edmund Wilson honored Houdini's authority. The son of a rabbi, Houdini pursued his studies with rabbinic thoroughness. And, from the beginning of his career, he sought out the living legends of magic and badgered them in retirement, sometimes with tragicomic results.

As far back as 1895 it seemed to Houdini something peculiar was going on when he performed the Metamorphosis with his wife, Bess. You have probably seen this classic illusion. Two friends of mine once acted it in my living room, as a birthday present. When the Houdinis performed the Metamorphosis, Bess would handcuff Harry, tie him in a sack and lock him in a trunk. She would draw a curtain hiding the trunk and then it would open, showing Houdini free upon the stage. Where was Bess? Inside the trunk, inside the sack, handcuffed—there was Bess. The method of this trick is only mysterious if you cannot pay for it. But the Houdinis' *timing* of the Metamorphosis got very mysterious indeed. They polished the act until it happened in under three seconds, three rather blurred seconds in their own minds to be sure. Believe me, you cannot get *into* the trunk in under three seconds. So when the Houdinis had done the trick they were often as stunned as their audience. It seemed a sure case of technique unleashing a supernatural force. Perplexed, Houdini planned to interview Herrmann the Great, the preeminent conjuror in America in 1895, and ask Herrmann what was up. But Herrmann died as Houdini was about to ask him the question.

And Houdini shadowed the marvelous Harry Kellar, cross-examining him, and Alexander Heimburger, and the decrepit Ira Davenport, who had been a medium as well as a magician. But the great magicians flatly denied the psychic possibility, and Davenport would not answer to Houdini's satisfaction. In 1903 he discovered that Wiljalba Frikell, a seemingly mythic wizard of the nineteenth century, was still alive, in retirement near Dresden. When the ancient sage would not acknowledge his letters, Houdini grew convinced Wiljalba Frikell was the man to answer his question. He took the train to Dresden and knocked on Frikell's door. His wife sent Houdini away. On the road in Germany and Russia, Houdini continued to send letters and gifts to Frikell. And at last, six months after he had been turned away from Frikell's door, the reclusive magician agreed to see him.

Houdini rang the doorbell at two p.m. on October 8, 1903, the exact hour of his appointment. The door swung open. An hour earlier Wiljalba Frikell had dressed in his best suit, and laid out his scrapbooks, programs and medals for Houdini to view. Houdini excitedly followed Frikell's wife into the room where the master sat surrounded by the mementos of his glorious career. But he would not be answering any of the questions that buzzed in Houdini's brain. The old man was stone dead.

Throughout his life Houdini categorically denied that any of his effects were achieved by supernatural means. He crusaded against mediums, clairvoyants and all who claimed psychic power, advertising that he would reproduce any of their manifestations by mechanical means. In the face of spiritualists who accused *him* of being a "physical medium", he protested that all his escapes and illusions were tricks. He was probably telling the truth, as he understood it. But Rabbi Drachman, who spoke at Houdini's funeral and had been in a position to receive confidences, said: "Houdini possessed a wondrous power that he never understood, and which he never revealed to anyone in life."

Houdini was not Solomon; he was a vaudeville specialist. If he ever experienced a psychic power it surely humbled his understanding. And to admit such a power, in his position, would have been a monumental stupidity. Why? If for no other reason, Talmudic law forbids the performance of miracles, and Houdini was the obedient son of Rabbi Weiss. Also, in case he should forget the Jewish law, it is strictly against the magician's code to claim a supernatural power, for reasons impossible to ignore. Mediums made such claims at their own risk. Two of the more famous mediums of the nineteenth century, Ira and William Davenport, achieved manifestations similar to Houdini's. Audiences in Liverpool, Leeds and Paris rioted, stormed the stage and ran the mediums out of town, crying their performances were an outrage against God and a danger to man. Whether or not the acts were supernatural is beside the point—billing them as such was bad business, and hazardous to life and limb. Yet the Davenports were no more than a sideshow, compared to Houdini. The man was blinding. There had not been such a public display of apparent miracles in nearly two thousand years. Had the Jew so much as hinted his powers were spiritual he might have expected no better treatment than the renegade Hebrew of Nazareth.

Houdini was the self-proclaimed avatar of nothing but good old American know-how, and that is how he wished to be remembered. His wife of thirty years, Beatrice Houdini, was loyal to him in this, as in all other things. Pestered for revelations about Houdini's magic long after his death, the widow swore by her husband's account. But against her best intentions, Bess clouded the issue by saying a little more than was necessary in a letter to Sir Arthur Conan Doyle.

The friendship between the Houdinis and Doyle was an odd one. The creator of Sherlock Holmes believed in spiritualism, and championed the séance with all the fervor that Houdini opposed it. There were two great mysteries in Doyle's life: the powers of Sherlock Holmes and Harry Houdini. Doyle knew the Houdinis intimately, and nothing the magician said could shake Sir Arthur's conviction that certain of Houdini's escapes were supernatural. Doyle never stopped trying to get Houdini to confess. In 1922 it was more than a personal issue. The séance had become big business in America, with millions of bereaved relatives paying to communicate with their dear departed. Spiritualism was a homegrown, persuasive religious movement, a bizarre reaction to American science and pragmatism. The great critic Edmund Wilson, who admired Houdini and understood his gifts, recognized the magician had appeared at a critical moment in the history of spiritualism. Houdini was the only man living who had the authority, and the competence, to expose the predatory mediums, and his success was decisive.

Yet Houdini's lecture-demonstrations, and exposures of false mediums, only fueled Doyle's suspicions that his friend was the real thing, a "physical medium". In all fairness, Sir Arthur Conan Doyle was a credulous old gentleman who knew nothing of Houdini's techniques. But his instinct was sound. Two months after Houdini died, Sir Arthur wrote to

Beatrice in despair of ever learning the truth from the magician's lips, and she wrote Doyle a long letter. What concerns us here are a few sentences which, coming from the woman who shared his life and work, and maintained her loyalty to Houdini alive and dead, we must regard as altogether startling.

> I will never be offended by anything you say for him or about him, but that he possessed psychic powers—he never knew it. As I told Lady Doyle often he would get a difficult lock, I stood by the cabinet and I would hear him say, "This is beyond me," and after many minutes when the audience became restless I nervously would say, "Harry, if there is anything in this belief in Spiritualism,—why don't you call on them to assist you," and before many minutes had passed Houdini had mastered the lock.
>
> We never attributed this to psychic help. We just knew that particular instrument was the one to open that lock, and so did all his tricks.

The tone of this letter penned so soon after her husband's death is somber throughout, painfully sincere. This was not a subject for levity, this being the central issue in the life of Harry Houdini. So what on earth is Bess trying to tell Sir Arthur when she testifies to the invocation of spirits, in one sentence, and repudiates psychic help in the next? What kind of double talk is this, when the widow refers to the summoning of spiritual aid as "that particular instrument," as if a spirit were no different from any other skeleton key? It sounds like sheer euphemism; it sounds like the Houdinis' lifetime of work had uncovered a power so terrifying they would not admit it to each other, let alone the world. Would that Albert Einstein had been so discreet in 1905.

So what if Harry Houdini, once in a while, "spirited" himself out of a Siberian van, or a pair of *Mirror* handcuffs, or a packing case at the bottom of the East River? It is perhaps no more remarkable than an American Jew winning a verdict against the German police for criminal libel in 1901, or reversing a religious movement in America in 1922. Houdini died in Detroit on Halloween of 1926, of acute appendicitis. He was born in Budapest on March 24, 1874, but told the world he was born in Appleton, Wisconsin, on April 6. Not until after World War II did Americans discover that their greatest magician was an alien. Houdini's work was no more miraculous than his life. His life was no more miraculous than the opening and closing of a flower.

The Great
American Ghost

Toward the stroke of midnight on Halloween, a crowd will gather in the monumental shades of the graveyard in Baltimore where Edgar Allan Poe lies buried. His tombstone casts a long shadow. From its granite base the veined Italian marble rises two heads taller than any celebrant. On one panel of the tombstone, the author of "The Tell-Tale Heart" gazes out from a medallion portrait ornamented with acanthus leaves and a lyre wreathed with laurel, the emblems of his professional immortality. Poe lives and summons a crowd every Halloween. He is truly the man who owns midnight.

Each member of the crowd has his or her own connection with the storyteller, the poet, and his work. Many are grateful for his invention of the detective story, in which ideas, more than pistols, bring criminals to justice. Some will come to pay tribute to the poet, who sang so hauntingly of a dead woman and a paradise that was always just out of reach. But by far the greatest number of people will come to honor a debt they cannot repay, a debt of terror. As children, they were terrified by Poe's tales of madness and premature burial and pathological murder. He seems to have inhabited a nightmare to which young people are tenderly susceptible. Most of the crowd would admit they have outgrown the fears of childhood but cannot forget them, or the author that fanned those fears into a bonfire.

But no one is likely to tell you the deeper reason that they will gather in this graveyard on Halloween, the night when goblins and spirits are licensed to roam the town. Edgar Allan Poe is a Great American Ghost. With the crowd's instinct for centralization, they will gather at the most likely place, at the perfect time, to experience an apparition. If there are ghosts, Poe is certainly one of them. And if ghosts make public appearances, it will be from this source, at this most hospitable hour. Poe loved publicity, and if there were any way he could oblige us, he would.

What makes a Great American Ghost? Who qualifies? One must be an American, first of all, and one must be dead. Yet there are too many souls who satisfy these requirements for all of them to haunt us; in this most democratic of nations, democracy has little influence among the dead. You must not only be dead and an American, you must be great as well. And even that is not enough.

Take George Washington, for instance. No crowd of ghostwatchers will gather at Mount Vernon on Halloween, because George Washington, for all his decisive greatness, and deadness, is not likely to haunt anyone but a few guilty presidents. His life was full, and wholesome for the most part. From all indications the Father of Our Country was well-suited for living among the living. He flourished so completely into his seventh decade that when he died of pneumonia, in his bed, he was able to bid farewell to the world and make a clean break from it, without a second glance.

Now let us return to the tomb of Edgar Allan Poe, Great American Ghost. Everything about Poe's birth, death and progress through this world is so marked by frustration and downright eeriness you would think that Poe was intended for life in some realm other than ours. Consider the handsome tombstone of veined Italian marble. Poe was a proud man, and his greatness did not deliver him from vanity. He dressed like a Victorian dandy, except in death, when poverty forced upon him the castoff vest and neckcloth of the medical students who prepared him for his journey. All the more reason Poe would be delighted with a fine tombstone, which might compensate for the insult of his final attire. You can imagine him, the color of twilight, pacing around his fresh grave, grumbling about his ill-fitting coat and trousers and awaiting delivery of the tombstone that might restore his dignity.

He had to wait twenty-five years. Other people died and were buried around him, mourned by loving relatives who erected noble monuments in memoriam. Not Poe. First his unfashionably dressed corpse lay in the rotunda of Washington College Hospital while newspapermen, acquaintances and curious readers gaped at him. They asked for locks of the poet's hair, and there was not enough to go around. So many came to gaze at the dead author that the funeral was postponed for days. Yet few came to see him buried on a cloudy afternoon in October of 1849, and no one would pay for a tombstone.

Ten years later Judge Neilson Poe, a cousin, commissioned a marble slab from a stonemason. Hugh Sisson chiseled Poe's name and an epigram in faulty Latin and carried the stone into his yard to rest with several others that were awaiting delivery. The mason's yard was conveniently located on the tracks of the Northern Central Railroad. A freight train locomotive steaming through Sisson's stoneyard leapt the tracks and, as if it despised faulty Latin, smashed Poe's tombstone to powder, leaving the others intact.

Poe may have had a shadowy hand in this. As anxious as he might have been to see his funeral arrangements completed, Poe was a fine Latin scholar and an all-out perfectionist. An ungrammatical tombstone would not have sat well on him. But imagine the frustration of his spirit when Judge Poe, bowing to fate, failed to renew his order for the stone. Another fifteen years dragged on before a group of schoolteachers collected enough money to honor the poet with a monument, a project that many writers and critics resisted in the distasteful memory of Poe's behavior when drinking and his sometimes brusque treatment of colleagues. But the schoolteachers raised the money and commissioned sculptor Sir Moses Ezekiel.

Sir Moses straightaway created a clay model of the monument and sent it to the foundry to be cast. There a fire destroyed it. Sir Moses, undaunted, pounded together a second model of Poe's monument. The sculptor was putting the finishing touches on the model when an earthquake shook the clay to pieces, along with the studio that housed it. Sir Moses survived. And in the knowledge that luck comes in threes, he hastily refashioned Poe's monument and, before it could be struck by lightning, had it cast and delivered to the cemetery where it now stands, to the relief of Poe's spirit.

To be a Great American Ghost, you must lead a life characterized by frustration and eeriness, like the story of Edgar Allan Poe's monument. The poet's whole life was like that. He dwelt among ghosts. Both of his parents acted on the stage, and one would not be surprised to learn that Poe's mother was playing the haunted Ophelia or Cordelia, possibly just months before the poet's birth in Boston. Shortly thereafter, his father disappeared, never to be seen again by mother or son, except in dreams. Five years later Poe's mother was dead of consumption.

Having grown up with ghosts of his mother and father, the young Poe naturally fell in love with a girl half-dead of consumption, his cousin Virginia Clemm. He married Virginia when she was thirteen and lived with the dying woman for most of his adult life. She suffocated at twenty-four, the same age at which Poe's mother died. The poet placed his wife's casket on his writing table. Some artist sketched the only portrait we have of the dead woman, in her white linen gown, the serene oval of her face, the flickering smile. The closed eyelids of the sketch were later painted open for a more cheerful effect, but they remain strangely lifeless. Wrapped in the cloak that had comforted his dying wife, Poe followed her down an alley of funereal trees to the graveyard.

The inconsolable poet could not leave the graveyard. According to one contemporary account, by C.C. Burr, a friend of Poe's, "Many times after the death of his beloved wife, was he found at the dead hour of a winter night, sitting beside her tomb almost frozen in the snow, where he had wandered from his bed weeping and wailing." Poe was thirty-eight years old and would become a ghost himself two years later. It was as if he were in training for the role.

The frustrations of Poe's literary career are legendary and without parallel. If the world was hard on him, he was even harder on himself, setting literary standards above any known to his contemporaries. He toiled incessantly from the age of seventeen to perfect a style that yielded masterpieces in every genre known in his time. Not satisfied with that, he invented a new one, the mystery story. His genius was recognized when he was only twenty-four, when he won a prize for the story "MS. Found in a Bottle." Despite ill health and grinding poverty, he produced an astonishing body of work. To argue that he was misunderstood is a gross oversimplification. The editors and critics of his time understood Poe all too well; let it suffice to say his brilliance incited such envy and malice that lesser men worked to destroy him, a labor speeded by the poet's brain lesion and his pathetic allergy to alcohol. The passing of his child-bride, Virginia, hastened the ultimate circumstance that confirmed Poe as a Great American Ghost: a violent and painful death.

A great deal of nonsense has been written about Poe's last days that does no credit to the man or his ghost and is impertinent to our discussion. Six days before he died Poe was in Richmond, Virginia, preparing to depart for an editing job in Philadelphia. A friend recalled that the last time she saw him, waving goodby in her doorway, a meteor flashed in the sky over his head. Poe sailed for Baltimore, where he called on a friend, Dr. Nathan Brooks, who reported that the poet had been drinking. Then he disappeared for five days. Another friend, Dr. James Snodgrass, found Poe in a barroom, slumped unconscious in an armchair. He wrote that Poe was "haggard, bloated and unwashed." Poe appeared to be wearing someone else's clothing, which indicated foul play. Snodgrass took the poet to the hospital, where he lay in a coma until three o'clock the next morning.

Edgar Allan Poe awoke from his coma to a violent trembling of his limbs and an unrelieved delirium. Drenched in sweat, the poet spoke animatedly with people and objects he envisioned on the walls of his hospital room. For a day and a half he was so distracted and violent that relatives were not allowed in the room. When he calmed down briefly during the second day, Dr. J. J. Moran attempted conversation and discovered that the poet was lost in time. Moran later reported that Poe spoke of a dreamed marriage as if it had occurred, and had no knowledge of recent events. When Moran tried to console Poe with hopes for his recovery the poet renewed his violence saying, "The best thing my best friend could do would be to blow out my brains with a pistol." He was looking for mercy from the wrong quarter. Moran left the room, and when he returned a few minutes later he discovered Poe in such a violent state it took two nurses to restrain him. For two days the poet raved in delirium against an invisible enemy, screaming the name of someone called "Reynolds" whose identity remains a mystery. At last, exhausted, Poe mumbled, "Lord, help my poor soul," and departed this life.

The imperfect medical knowledge of the time does not provide us with a satisfactory cause of death. But the eyewitness accounts suggest that Poe's delicate heart burst under the pressure of a fright that may have equaled the composite effect of his tales upon a generation of readers.

What was he struggling against that it took two nurses to hold him down? Was it death? Is it possible that a man who had lived his entire life in the company of ghosts, to a point of seeming to converse with them in his last hours, would be afraid of becoming a ghost at last? It seems more likely that the man who had lived with one foot in the next world all of his life had a vision that his frustration and pain would not end at death's door. He may have thought that his suffering would increase, that he would be doomed to live half in and half out of life eternally, as a Great American Ghost.

There may be a few members of the crowd at Poe's grave on Halloween who have vivid imaginations. These will search the monumental shadows and tremble, remembering their horror at reading Poe's nightmare story "The Premature Burial." There in the shadows or in their mind's eye, which is Poe's world, they may see a tormented poet the color of twilight, no more alive or dead now than he was in 1844, when he wrote the immortal tale.

The Star-Spangled Banner

T he Star-Spangled Banner" is a sublime anthem, democratic and spacious, holding at least one note for every
American, but too many for any solitary singer. The tune is a
test pattern, not only for the voice, but for the human spirit.
The soul singer, the rock star and the crooner—all are humbled by the anthem. We have heard world-famous tenors and
sopranos choke upon the low notes, and cry out in pain at the
high ones. We have seen the great Mahalia Jackson tremble.

It is unlikely that our worst enemy would have written a
melody with a range more challenging to the solo performer. The melody *was* in fact given to us, like the Trojan
horse, by our worst enemy at the time, the English. John
Stafford Smith, an Englishman, composed the tune to which
Francis Scott Key penned his lyrics a few days after the
British set fire to our capital in 1814. The capital was rebuilt
but the melody remains exactly as we received it—an inspiration and a terror. The anthem perfectly suits our collective
spirit, our ambition and national range. So it ought to be
sung by a crowd of Americans, who may guarantee that all
of the notes will be covered.

You may wonder how the national anthem achieved its
election in the first place. And why, since the tune is so un-
cooperative, we can't impeach and throw the anthem out of
office, like any other incompetent or mischievous official? If
you are thinking such thoughts you are in good patriotic

company. The House Resolution 14, which legalized the national anthem, was voted down when it was first introduced in 1929, and hotly debated in 1931, when it did pass. Every few years since, there has been an uprising, with newspaper editorials, petitions against the song and insurgents campaigning to replace "The Banner" with "America" or "This Land Is Your Land."

If you are fond of "The Star-Spangled Banner," as most of us arc, the way folks will love a cantankerous grandfather, you may rest assured there are no new arguments likely to unseat or reform the anthem. Everything that could be said on the subject was said, over and over, during those debates of more than fifty years ago. Congressmen brought dire charges against "The Star-Spangled Banner." They denounced its ancestry, its birth and character. They dug up all the song's dirtiest secrets, ancient indiscretions, the follies of a wild and adventurous youth. They dragged "The Star-Spangled Banner" through the mud.

First of all there was that embarrassing business about the Anacreontic Society. We know that Francis Scott Key did not get his tune from a virgin inspiration. He wrote only the words; the melody had been married before, to the lyrics of an English song called "To Anacreon in Heaven," which made a very different kind of anthem indeed. The ancient Greek poet Anacreon delighted in wine and lovemaking above all else. In the 1770s, the London "gentlemen" of the Anacreontic Society chose the poet for their patron, and spent nights reviving his spirit with songs, and tippling, and unspecified merrymaking.

There were other problems as well. The congressmen against the "Banner" claimed that the song was useless on the parade and battle grounds because our soldiers cannot march to it. To this charge there seems to be no answer. Yet John Philip Sousa, who should have known, once told Teddy Roosevelt that "The Star Spangled Banner" was dandy for marching. Perhaps the soldiers had not tried hard enough. After all, any fool army could march to the "Marseillaise" or "God Save the Queen," but who but an American army could get in step to "The Star-Spangled Banner"? And finally, if our soldiers cannot march to "The Star-Spangled Banner," they cannot dance to it either. Better that it does not lend itself to any kind of frivolity. In fact you can do little with the anthem but listen to it, and only with great difficulty, since the song is nearly impossible to sing.

This brings us to the next argument against "The Star Spangled Banner": that it is too difficult for school children to sing. An editorial in the New York *World* of March 31, 1930, answered this charge with logic and eloquence: "What if school children could sing it? We should be so sick of it by now that we could not endure the sound of it, as the French are sick of the 'Marseillaise.' The virtues of 'The Star-Spangled Banner' are that it does require a wide compass, so that school children cannot sing it, and that it is in three–four time so that parades cannot march to it. So being, it has managed to remain fresh, not frayed and worn, and the citizenry still hear it with some semblance of a thrill, some touch of reverence."

To the *World*'s persuasive comments, we can only add that the school children of the Third Reich had an anthem they could sing and march to with the greatest of ease. It did them no good. An amusing irony of the congressional debates is that, while some lawmakers complained the "Banner" was unmarchable, others thought the lyrics were too warlike. A close reading of all four stanzas should reassure the doves. Far from advocating war, Key's words express the utmost horror of it, suiting the occasion that brought the song into being.

As for the occasion, the bombardment of Fort McHenry in 1814, a few congressmen suggested this was too paltry a background for our national anthem. They had not read their history. If the British had gotten into Baltimore, only a few days after burning down our capital, no one can say where they might have stopped. Who would have stopped them? George Washington had been dead fifteen years. Andrew Jackson was in New Orleans. If the British navy's offensive had not foundered at Fort McHenry we might be singing "God Save the Queen" instead of not singing "The Star Spangled Banner."

So, a half century ago, our anthem stood proud and unflinching and unrepentent while the lawmakers weighed it, prodded it and leered at it, examining its teeth and moral record. Perhaps the best argument against the House Resolution is that it was unnecessary, and therefore impertinent, rather like electing the turkey to be the Official Entrée of Thanksgiving. Way back in the nineteenth century Admiral Dewey designated "The Star Spangled Banner" as the anthem for all Navy ceremonies. And when advisers asked what song should accompany state functions in 1916, President Wilson automatically replied, "The Banner." Everybody knew it was the national anthem.

But Americans do not like to be told what to eat, or drink, or sing. Though they have eaten hot dogs and drunk beer and sung "The Star-Spangled Banner" in baseball parks for generations, try to pass a law to that effect and Congress will never hear the end of it. That is the American way, and a good way. When Representative J. C. Linthicum of Maryland agitated to make "The Star-Spangled Banner" our *official* anthem, he might have foreseen he would be subjecting the "Banner" to a scrutiny usually reserved for presidential candidates. The final vote to give the song official status as our national anthem, despite its vocal challenges, unmarchability and checkered past, is a gesture of American affection without precedent or parallel.

"The Star-Spangled Banner" deserves it. That insuperable anthem remains the purest example of unpremeditated, inspired genius in American history. Remember that Francis Scott Key, the lawyer poet, was more lawyer than poet. Apart from the lyrics of "The Banner" Key never wrote a line of memorable verse, . . . excepting "Lord with Glowing Heart I'd Praise Thee," a hymn infrequently sung in churches. Francis Scott Key was tone deaf. If anyone had told him early in September of 1814 that he was about to write the most famous song in America, the lawyer poet would have laughed, with a modesty rare in poets, and gone about his business.

Key's business in September of 1814 was a matter of life and death. America had declared war upon slender pretexts the lawyer poet condemned as a cover for imperialism. American privateers were looting British ships, and our troops had set Toronto on fire in the interest of annexing Canada. Not to be outdone, the British burned down Washington, D.C. Key was a gentle soul, so unsuited to conflict he could never bring himself to run for political office. Yet he fought dutifully in the defense of Washington. And when the British took away a civilian prisoner, Dr. William Beanes,

Daniel Mark Epstein

Key begged for President Madison's commission to sail after them, and plead for the doctor's release.

Key sailed down the Chesapeake in a small cartel ship, under the white flag of truce. He found the British fleet lying at anchor in the mouth of the Potomac. Admiral George Cockburn was about to hang Dr. Beanes from the ship's yardarm for his inhospitality to English soldiers as they passed through Upper Marlboro. The doctor had been having a garden party to celebrate the town's escape from burning, when a few straggling dragoons came into his yard and made bold to steal the punch. Dr. Beanes had been court-martialed for not giving them any, among other discourtesies.

With the passion and eloquence of a great lawyer poet, Francis Scott Key pleaded for Dr. Beanes's life. The lawyer suggested that the strictest guardians of etiquette did not require a host to serve punch to the army of the occupation. Then he argued that the detaining of civilians outraged all principles of civilized warfare; if great nations cannot agree upon the principles of warfare, what on earth *could* they agree upon? Admiral Cockburn was unmoved. What finally swayed him were certain letters from his wounded soldiers, showing what tender care Dr. Beanes had taken of them. Key produced these letters from his satchel. After a heated conference the British officers announced they would release the ill-mannered doctor the next morning.

Key's mission was badly timed for all purposes but the creation of our anthem. That very night the British fleet received orders to attack Baltimore. Since they could not conceal this from Key, they insisted that he accept their hospitality until the battle was over, making him an offer he could not refuse. The British entertained the lawyer poet on his own cartel ship. From there he had an excellent view of the contest, being right in the middle of it.

Now let us pay tribute to Key's inspiration, which came in a moment bearing a song that must outlive every American. We have all known some inspiration, whether we write, or paint, or teach, or build houses. Inspiration is, above all, emotion. What was Francis Scott Key *feeling* as he watched the rockets' red glare, and the bombs bursting in air, and then saw the banner waving? He jotted notes on the back of an envelope. Later the lawyer poet would admit: "If it had been a hanging matter to make a poem, I must have made it." The reference to execution is not careless. It is more than likely that the gentle Key, in making his poem, was as terrified a lawyer poet as ever held a quill in his hand.

You singers who have been honored with an invitation to perform the anthem for a crowd, remember Key's terror and be comforted. Whatever indignities you may suffer from bungling "The Star-Spangled Banner," you are not likely to die from it. But in 1814, the rockets' red glare and bombs bursting in air were neither poetic fantasies nor Fourth of July fireworks. They were real, live bombs, screaming, and whistling, and exploding around the poet. Dr. Beanes, who had joined Key on the cartel's deck, must have thought he had been saved from hanging only to be blown up.

The British rocket, a kind of primitive guided missile, was an awesome innovation in 1814. Key had watched his own men panic under bombardment from those rockets during the defense of Washington, and probably figured the Baltimoreans would do the same. The lawyer poet must have had wildly mixed emotions as the British ships, and his country's own boat, approached the shore, beautifully lighted by rockets so that his fellow Americans could take better

Daniel Mark Epstein

aim at him with their cannons. We could hardly blame Key if he had prayed for a swift surrender. He did not. He wrote a poem instead, and prayed for a sight of the flag.

A word about the flag. It is not just any flag, the one that flew above Fort McHenry in 1814. It is arguably the largest battle flag ever flown, thirty-six feet long by twenty-nine feet wide, one hundred forty square yards of red, white and blue bunting. The flag was made to order for the defense of Fort McHenry, as well as the creation of our anthem. What else would possess General Stricker and Commodore Barney, otherwise reasonable men, to order such a gigantic banner? They wanted to be sure that Key would see it. Although the seamstress Mary Pickersgill snipped the stripes and stars in her tiny workroom, she could not stitch them together there. Mary and her little daughter worked on their hands and knees, by daylight and lamplight, stitching together the star-spangled banner on the malthouse floor of Claggett's brewery. They finished their sewing just as the British fleet was nearing the Baltimore harbor.

The flag is surrealistically large. If you do not believe this, then go and look at it, hanging like a dinosaur in the Smithsonian Institution's Museum of American History. That flag, flying above Fort McHenry, must have made the fort, and the city behind it, look like a child's sand castle. What was the author of our anthem feeling, after the long night of rockets and bomb blasts and horror, what was he feeling when he saw that titanic flag flying weirdly above his miniature homeland? Some would say relief. But it was too soon for Key to feel relief—he was still a prisoner of war. Some would say pride. But Key was famous for nothing but his humility; he was anecdotally humble. And besides, pride does not spring readily in one's breast so soon after courage has been shaken. After a night of unspeakable terror, with every reason to believe that America would surrender in the glare of the rockets, Francis Scott Key's emotion upon spying that bizarre flag must have been utter amazement.

Wonder is a better word. Key could not believe his eyes, and his lyrics reproduce in us that sense of wonder. Remember, the refrain that closes the first stanza is a question:

> O! say does that star-spangled banner yet wave,
> O'er the Land of the free, and the home of the brave?

When we sing the anthem in the ballpark, or in school, or before the fireworks display on July 4, it is altogether fitting that we sing no more of the lyrics after that question. The birth and survival of this nation remains one of the wonders of the world. This was never more evident than it was to the lawyer poet on that cloudy morning in 1814. The flag was amazing but undeniable. Key knew exactly how brave *he* was, having so recently been measured for bravery. Yet he still had sensible doubts about his freedom. That is the American way, and it is a good way.

My Father's Life

I have seen a photograph of him at the wheel of a racing car with the legend "Sneaky Pete" blazoned across its hood. With his sandpaper beard and furious brows, he looks like Robert de Niro in *Raging Bull*, but with no teeth. Nobody fed him properly, and his teeth rotted. As the story goes, my father had grown weary of the pain and pulled what was left of the teeth with a pair of pliers. He needed attention. Teeth and bones had been robbed of phosphorous at age three when his curiosity, unchecked, led him to pry the cap off a steam radiator, and for weeks he lay near death from the scalding. The scar on his abdomen was so inflexible that when I was a boy my father wore his belt buckle on his hip. So did I, unaware that what I imitated as style was his shift against pain.

In the photograph my father is grinning under a crash helmet. The date is 1943, five years before I was born, and my father was fifteen years old. He owned the racing car. He also owned a Lincoln convertible with a musical horn, a wardrobe that rivaled Sinatra's, and dental plates. His precocity beggars description. The unruly offspring of a failed marriage, my father caromed from one exasperated aunt to another until attaining his majority at age twelve. Then he set up bachelor quarters at the Hotel Houston in downtown Washington, D.C.

Looking for work, my father discovered a valuable knack

for fixing things. A kindly Greek who owned a route of pinball machines let him sleep under one of them. That was in the late thirties, when those who had spare change would drop it gladly into the ringing, flashing games so they might forget their troubles. The Greek was willing to pay a lot of money to keep the games ringing and flashing and my father was a prodigy at it. He worked long into the night fixing machines, after the arcades were closed.

So when he turned thirteen his income was in five figures. Called to the principal's office to discuss poor attendance and catnapping in classes, my father was well fortified with his own theories and proofs of education. After listening politely as the principal described the hardships of life without a diploma, my father asked what the man's salary would be in the coming week. The educator, either disarmed by the student's boldness, or hoping to win his confidence, told him. My father hauled from his oversized pocket a roll of banknotes, waved it in the man's face, and announced that he had made that much money *last night*. The principal called for some vice principal to see my father to the door of Mt. Rainier High School, which he did not enter again for twenty years, only then to see his son accept the Faculty Award for scholarship.

Education. I have heard him use that word more often, and with more reverence, than any other. Growing up on the street, with nothing but his own wits to protect him, my father nurtured an instinctive curiosity into a passion for learning. Had he been born into a comfortable middle-class Jewish home, he might have become a doctor or an engineer. Delivered into the anarchy and illiteracy of the streets, he became a mechanic. It is not hard to imagine him as a boy, breaking into the Greek's pinball machine, not to steal the nickels, just hungry to analyze this contraption that made bells ring and numbers flash, and men line up to drop their coins in that generous stream.

Fathers teach their sons what they know best. When I was old enough to go to work for him, my father had his own amusement arcade. The green neon sign in the window over the hot dog stand said PLAYLAND. He taught me to fix lame flippers and jammed coin shoots on the pinball machines. A tattoo artist flourished in a wire cage beyond the end of the bar where hunting knives and stilettos glittered in a display case. On Saturdays I rode the bus downtown to go to "work," a word my father used interchangeably with the word "education." I worked the cash register. I worked the floor, wearing a green moneybelt, making change.

In the early sixties my father moved most of the pinball games out of the arcade, to make room for a book shelf. The wire journal rack that stocked the racing forms and detective magazines could not meet the demand for men's literature that followed the notorious banning of *Tropic of Cancer*. The fifth page of Henry Miller's novel, which seems tame now, was incendiary in those days. And when it became required reading for every American man, woman, teenager, priest and policeman, nobody in the nation's capital had the book but the vice squad and my father.

As we stocked the shelves with Miller's novels and the complete line from Grove Press, including Genet, Beckett and Burroughs, the Playland became not only the center for the propagation of adult fantasies, but the single source of avant-garde literature in Washington, D.C. Retailing these masterpieces was not an aesthetic or even a political impulse on my father's part, not at the time. Later the government would awaken him to his responsibilities vis-à-vis the First

Amendment. At first it was simply good business; the books were selling like wildfire.

The books sold so well that by the time I was in high school, the former pinball mechanic was commanding a suite of offices above the Playland with five secretaries, two accountants and dozens of managers. When I was considering colleges, one afternoon my father ordered everybody out of his office so he could talk to me alone.

"You can go to any college in America," he said. "You have the grades, and I have the money. But you have to promise me two things. First of all, you'll continue to work for me every summer. I don't want college to interfere with your education. Second, you've got to promise me you won't become a writer or a schoolteacher."

I looked straight into his eyes and I lied to him. I was not sure I was lying to him, because I had lied to myself first to make it easier. I wanted to go to college more than anything, and I knew he would not send me if I told him I was going there to fulfill my dream of becoming a writer. All the writers my father knew were bums. So I told him I did not know what I wanted to be. And I half believed it myself, though he never did. I told him I was going to study law, which was what he had begun to do, spending his free afternoons in the criminal courts the way some men sneak off to the golf course or the movies. Had he been born into a middle-class Jewish home he might have become an attorney. Delivered into the paracriminal business world, with congressmen and police inspectors damning or praising his livelihood as it pleased their constituents, my father became an uncertified authority on criminal law and civil liberties. So I told him I was going to study law, a lie he wanted to believe.

And I went on lying to him after matriculating at Kenyon College, after studying Shakespeare and Browning, Lawrence and the Classical Greeks, those heroes of literature and philosophy I could not help but emulate. I lied to him during the summers when I managed his bookstore and burlesque house in Dayton, composing poems secretly. My father would introduce me to his new friends, famous first amendment attorneys, saying proudly, "My son, the lawyer." And I would blush because I suspected it was a lie, and I had made him share it. I went right on lying until I graduated with highest honors in English, and a foundation grant to write a book. Then I told him the truth. I would not work for him that summer, or any other summer, because I had become a writer.

For two years my father would not permit my name to be mentioned in his presence. I had lied to him. And I had accepted his money to become educated in a field which to him was contemptible, if not wholly irrelevant. The responsibility of a grown man, he believed, was to take care of himself, his family and his friends, in a world that showed neither mercy nor sympathy for those too stupid to protect themselves. A man must make as much money as he possibly can without breaking the law, and then use the money wisely and charitably. Only the most diligent correspondence on my part, and my mother's diplomacy, brought us together again. And it was none too soon for either of us.

In the midseventies my father was arraigned on sixty-six counts of conspiracy to violate the laws of interstate commerce by transporting obscene materials across the state line. This was not the first time he had been called to account. Local authorities had been hounding him for years in several states, as it suited the electorate; and though my father was most scrupulous in observing the diverse obscenity codes, he had been tried again and again, at great cost, without a conviction.

But this was a federal case. The F.B.I. had conducted the investigation and the arrest, there was a Republican in the White House and my father could go to jail for a long time. I began commuting to Washington from my home in Baltimore to attend my father, and his trial, which he regarded with his usual good humor and bravado, though he had drawn a judge known to be unsympathetic to his cause, and a jury that looked like the cast of *Annie Get Your Gun*. One day I brought him a newspaper with a feature story on his son, the writer, the headline: "Poetry His Aim—Short of Starvation." I thought it might cheer him up, and it did. He loved it.

I sat in a conference room and watched my father, overweight and pale, presiding over the attorneys. He was wearing his narrow blue "courtroom" tie, which he hated, and sat calmly at the head of a long table. There were three criminal lawyers, three first amendment lawyers and five professional witnesses, mostly authors and psychiatrists who would testify as to the nature of obscenity. I was the only person in the room that my father was not paying a thousand dollars a day to defend him. He was briefing the attorneys. This was a difficult case because of the explicit nature of the materials and the circumstances of their seizure, so both the criminal *and* the obscenity charges would have to be proven. My father, with his seventh-grade education, was lecturing these men and women on points of law and issues of morality so subtle and profound that John Milton and the Supreme Court itself had not gotten to the bottom of them.

They were questioning him, and hanging on his every word. The veteran of a dozen obscenity trials, he knew the answers because his life depended upon it.

I sat in that federal courtroom for weeks listening to the lawyers lose themselves in theory about the dangers of images and the rights of free citizens, until I knew my father was innocent whether he went to prison or not. And when at last the jury returned with their verdict of not guilty, it seemed not so much a judgment of him as an admission of their own bewilderment, as if they had been called to arbitrate a dispute for which their education had not prepared them. The only man in the building who really understood obscenity was the defendant, who was bound by the law of the land not to testify. My father had been pacing the corridor in measured steps, weary from awaiting their verdict, having broken his bank account, his health and all but his spirit to teach us what he knew best.

Making the Team

In a place of honor on the wall of my father's office there is a photograph of a young man smiling for all he is worth, as if to burst the knot of his tie. His hair, cropped close at the sides, partly accounts for the impression that the man's neck is wider than his head.

It is the head of a warrior. The first time my wife saw this portrait, she gasped. Alarmed at the family resemblance, she pointed to the face and asked my father who it might be. Proudly he told her the portrait was of his only son, her husband, in his days of glory.

Now I am not going into any detail about how my looks have changed since I was sixteen. It is enough to say that my head has remained more or less the same size, but my neck has shrunk, so the tie chafing that young man's throat would now dangle upon mine like a necklace. Normal living has restored my neck to its rightful size; what swelled it like an angry cobra's at sixteen was high school football.

The heavy-duty, industrial-weight neck was clearly not ornamental. It served the vital function of keeping my head attached to my shoulders when mammoth linebackers wanted so badly to dislodge it. I would be carrying the football out of the backfield, and while one of them was tackling me and another was trying to seize the football, which I had been taught not to give up, a third would try to take my head away from me. The helmet I wore for protection was conveniently equipped with a face bar the villain could grab to facilitate the business, so nothing stood between me and decapitation but a colossal and unyielding neck.

You might ask yourself why I had placed myself in that position. My wife has asked me that. My father never asked. He did not play high school football, but he took up boxing at about the same age. My father trained informally at Mack Lewis' gym, in Washington, D.C., and used to spar with Billy Conn. Out of the goodness of his heart Billy Conn did not kill my father; Conn played with the amateur as a cat plays with a mouse. My father survived to teach me how to box. He began the lessons in boxing after the first time I came crying about the neighborhood bully, and on more than one occasion since then the science has been more precious to me than grammar, or physics. My father never asked me why I wanted to play football because he assumed it was for the same reason he wanted to get in the ring with Billy Conn, and that football was just a more social and inelegant form of boxing, for groups rather than individuals.

When I was in high school the single incontrovertible evidence of manhood was making the varsity football squad. It was not getting the driver's license, or success in love, or even making the basketball, baseball or track team. These achievements were within the grasp of everyone, and often attained by males whose status was questionable. But making the football team placed one's manhood beyond discussion. Here was power, fame and glory, the crowd's applause and the adoration of half-dressed cheerleaders who danced and screamed to keep warm. There was the serenading of brass bands, sports columnists and smooth recruiters from university athletic departments. Some laureled heroes even ascended to The Pros.

Out of fourteen hundred males in my high school, I suspect that twelve hundred would have sold their souls to the devil to make the football team. Four out of five of these disqualified themselves because of size, academic conflicts, physical infirmities and sheer terror. That left two hundred able and courageous souls determined to be among the thirty-three elect.

For the two hundred braves who showed up in the sweltering heat of August to try out, this was not the beginning. High school tryouts were the climax of a drama whose early acts were played in our grade-school years. Since the sport in its pure form was considered too dangerous for children, we were only allowed to play touch football in the schoolyard. But on our own time, we played full contact tackle, with no holds barred. There was no force on earth that could stop us, not our parents' admonishments, not our lack of equipment, neither rain nor snow nor our own bruises. When we could shout up enough recruits we would choose teams and scrimmage. When there were only a few of us we would play Murder-the-man-with-the-ball. In this variation the ball-carrier runs away from the company, or through them, as they try to put his nose in the dirt. When he is down he may toss the ball to any standing player, and the action resumes; or he may "eat the ball," a more dignified course of action, curling around the pigskin in a fetal position while the company, one by one, leaps on him until there is a writhing pile of torsos, arms and legs, like the Laocoön. This makes for a restful pause in the action, punctuated by groans, and cries, and the occasional snapping of a rib. I don't know how it is today, but when I was ten years old, boys' ribs were nearly unbreakable.

A few boys would join little-league football teams. But the

more structured situation could only refine what we had learned as children, running against each other in vacant lots. We learned to block and tackle, to pass and catch the football. Most important we learned when to run around an opponent and when to run over him, which is the evaluation of one's strength and courage. There are men you run around and then there are men you must run over, if you can; not to run over a tackler when it is both possible and necessary is a failure of nerve.

Of the neighborhood boys with whom I learned these fundamentals I was the most desperate, if not the strongest, and the only one who would try out for high school football. The desperation went deep. My father was away from home most of the time and I lacked a certain confidence that might have come of his presence. I wore glasses, and read too many books, which I feared would enervate me to a point of helplessness. Above all I wanted to be "well-rounded." It was the great age of the well-rounded youth, the post-World War II answer to the Renaissance Man. The ideal was the captain of the football team who was also editor of the school newspaper, and valedictorian, and still found a few hours on the weekend to tutor disadvantaged children. Of course there was no such person in a school of three thousand, specialization having already worked its mischief on the dreams of the well-rounded, so we were all more or less frustrated with ourselves.

This frustration, along with a hundred other grievances, doubts and longings like my own, hovered above the gridiron on that steamy morning in August, when two hundred of us showed up for football tryouts. All were prepared. Each had run over most of his childhood companions. Each had done his pushups, and situps, and windsprints and drunk two milkshakes a day to put on weight. Some had shaved their heads like savages, lacking only the warpaint and spears. The shaved skull was said to ease the application of the helmet, but that was a lie. Nothing could make the helmet comfortable, and the Myrmidons shaved their heads for the sole purpose of terrifying the rest of us.

The tryouts were conducted, for the first few days, by the veterans, the upperclassmen who had played football the year before. Two hundred of us were competing for twenty places—fifteen were already occupied by the veterans, some of whom wore their letter jackets despite the intense heat. These men looked down on the rest of us from a great eminence, out of the corners of their eyes, their muscles bulging, their buttressed heads, far from being shaved, groomed with an unembarrassed excess of confidence.

After enrolling our names on a roster, the veterans' first responsibility was to lead us in running laps around the field, and in calisthenics. This they condescended to do in shifts so as not to tire themselves, for these activities went on all day. The calisthenics were not for our benefit. The pushups, deep kneebends, the situps and jumping jacks were far in excess of training requirements. Now and again a boy would begin to shine bright red, and grow dizzy, then pass out from heat prostration while a veteran screamed at him to get up. Other athletes heard voices, and saw visions. The veterans had been instructed to test the limits of our endurance, and measure our desire to enter the combat lists. There were too many candidates to review efficiently; they wanted to see how many of us would die. An impassive veteran with a clipboard drew a line through one name after another, as bodies were carried from the field.

Half of the boys would not return. It was a good thing,

because there was hardly enough equipment to outfit the rest of us for battle. We would be using the castoff equipment — helmets, shoulder pads, hip pads and football breeches from the locker room archives. Many of the pads were museum pieces in need of restoration. Some were strapless, some laceless. There were helmets with visible fractures, and wingless shoulder pads. The veterans poured these into a pile in the middle of the locker room and let us pick and choose. It was every man for himself, and our first taste of combat. The strong and the swift would emerge with a full suit of armor, more or less the right size. Most of us would barter, and wrangle, and trade, and some would stumble out of the locker room like hunchbacked toreadors, under warped shoulder pads, or oversized helmets that slipped down over their eyes, blinding them. Most pathetic were those with helmets too small, for they would suffer headaches, and double vision, which is especially unsettling for a ball-carrier confronted by a heavyweight tackle.

Now we were ready for the "hitting," which is what we had all come for. One-on-one contact between ball-carriers and linemen was the focus of the whole tryout process, and we would spend days at it. The veterans separated us: the candidates for backfield, ball-carrying positions assembled on one side of the gridiron, and the candidates for guard or defensive positions gathered on the other. The jousting ground was an alley of the gridiron ten yards wide that ran from one side of the field to the other. A running back would be handed the ball and run full speed toward the lineman coming from the opposite direction. The ball-carrier's goal was to get around the tackler without stepping out of bounds, by dodging him or knocking him over. The tackler's job was to knock the ball-carrier down, or out of bounds. The alley's narrowness made collision nearly inevitable, and there was no loss of honor on either side as long as the "hitting" was direct, solid, and resonant.

The sound of leather on leather is as sweet to a football player's ears as the crack of a bat to a baseball player's. If you have not played football with helmets and padding, you may not fully appreciate the chief pleasure of the sport. It is not scoring touchdowns, or kicking or passing, which are the spectator's delights. The central and most intense pleasure of football is this "hitting." The comparison to hitting a baseball is not casual. When the baseball is hit solidly there is a harmonious sensation in the wooden handle that is precisely the same as what is felt in the head and shoulder of a tackler or blocker in the instant of contact, and in the cranium of a running back when he has used it to knock over his opponent. There is nothing else on earth like it, unless it is the knockout punch, which carries with it a sad note of finality. Solid contact in football is exhilarating, being both a distinct thrill in itself and an incitement to further action.

I learned this, and more things about football and myself in those tryouts in the late-summer haze, than I have learned in any comparable period of my life. It was a time for dispelling illusions. Like any great sport, football must reveal one's character before building it. With all of our helmets and pads and ragged jerseys, we stood as naked as babies in the eyes of the coaches, who had learned to read character through the language of movement. If you had courage, everyone could see it. If you were slow you were slow, and would be overtaken. If you had imagination and grace of movement it would work to your advantage if you did not make too much of it.

Now I fancied myself a dazzling balletic halfback on the

order of Paul Hornung, who would feint, and dodge, and pirouette among seven would-be tacklers as they groped for him and banged into each other, falling over themselves to tackle empty air as the halfback streaked into the end zone. Among the neighborhood boys I was like Paul Hornung. And in daydreams I would fly around the right flank with my left arm stiffly extended, the ball under my right arm, my body at a forty-five degree angle to the ground, and bareheaded, like a halfback in a magazine.

One-on-one contact speedily convinced me of the folly of that vision. Ten seconds in a narrow lane running against a capable lineman is no time for dancing. The first time I was handed the ball, I started toward my opponent running full tilt, grim and determined. He was taller than I was, and wider, and altogether cheerful-looking through his face mask. A third of the way along I changed my course and headed for the right sideline, intending to feint to the man's right, and depending upon his reflexes spin around his left side, or double back to his right. Midfield he just stopped and stood there, grinning. And while I was feinting, and fluttering, and gamboling, the man fixed his eyes on my naval, lowered his right shoulder and plowed right through me, driving me back twenty feet and pinning me to the ground. A great cheer went up from his colleagues at the other end of the field.

It was not any lack of nerve that had made me try to finesse my way around the tackler; it was rank ignorance. I had misunderstood the demands of the situation. The narrowness of the lane was greatly to the advantage of the tackler, and the ball-carrier's foremost asset was his momentum. It does not take a degree in physics to understand that any change in direction loses momentum, so any fakes, or pirouettes, or other tomfoolery, are an invitation to disaster for the ball-carrier, as they transform him from a dangerous projectile into a target. My sudden revelation was that the tackler, and not the ball-carrier, is the target in this situation, and that the more skillful runners were not getting *around* the tacklers; they seemed to be running overtop of them. It was weird, like an optical illusion. The ball-carrier would be running bolt upright, and the lineman would approach, stalking him. Just before contact the ball-carrier would lower his shoulder. You would hear a loud crack of helmets and the runner would be gone, leaving the lineman flat on his back.

I decided to work at this. I would cover the ball, over and under, with both arms, and run as fast as I could straight down the middle of the lane, looking into the eyes of my opponent. I learned there was a spot right around the man's sternum, and if I aimed my head at this spot just before contact, as the tackler bent to hug my thighs the butt of my helmet would knock his head back, and the rest of him would follow. It is one of the supreme satisfactions of youth. As a linebacker I have been on the receiving end of that exchange, and it is not so much painful as startling. One instant you are lunging for the ball carrier's thighs, certain of tackling him. And the next moment you are lying on the grass looking up at the sky.

I put this new knowledge directly in the service of my desire to make the football team. I was like a man possessed. Those lumbering guards were standing between me and the varsity immortals. It made me furious. I set my jaw, lowered my head, and with legs churning like pistons I ran them over. I was not particularly fast but I discovered an enormous drive, and I was utterly fearless because I had reduced the entire conflict to an abstraction. Never again would the relation between ambition and success be so elegantly expressed and so perfectly realized. There was the obstacle, the huge, bullet-headed lineman, and beyond him was the goal, the Varsity. In three days I must have run over forty or fifty men at least four times. At the end of the day my body was one limping bruise, and in the morning I was stiff as a corpse, but I was never happier. I began to notice that when my turn came to carry the football there would be a mysterious shuffling on the far side of the field, as the next victim discovered that his shoelace had come loose, or he was seized with a cramp in his thigh. This did not go unnoticed by the coaches.

So I found myself facing the same bulldogs over and over as our numbers dwindled. Each morning we would enter the locker room to look for our names on a list that was shrinking inexorably. Each day the survivors' equipment improved. I remember the combination of sadness and relief on the faces of the boys who could not find their names on the list. After looking again and again in vain, one would sigh. "Well"—swinging his duffel over his shoulder,—"guess I can go back to work at the garage." Or the ice cream parlor or the beach. For the defeated, the ordeal was over and they could lick their wounds in the shade, reclaiming the freedom of the last days of summer. One was rarely surprised at being cut, for each candidate had learned the true scope of his desire, and there was little else that determined his fate.

The last phase of the tryouts was the scrimmaging, with full teams of candidates going up against the veterans. But by then one could see that most of the decisions had been made. The men who had dominated the jousting were clearly the raw stuff from which football players would be molded. One by one they would cross over the scrimmage line to be tested in positions with the varsity veterans, while the rest remained on the defense to be used as "hamburger." I began running the fullback slot, carrying the ball in counter and off-tackle plays, and performed respectably, though I had not yet learned how to follow my blockers, and tended to run over them as well as everybody else.

When the final list was posted at the end of August I was one of five backfield players who would be joining the varsity team. I received a full complement of new equipment and a fresh blue jersey with the number 25 in white, with all the rights and privileges pertaining thereunto: a place of honor at pep rallies, a varsity jacket, a stack of party invitations, a harem of football groupies, and an aura of unchallengeable mettle which opened a path through crowded school hallways like the Red Sea parting for Moses.

Now I would like to tell you about how I rose from third-string fullback and linebacker to become a starter, a high school star, an All-American—but that was not to be. This had something to do with the character of the team. The football team fielded by Northwestern High School when I was an underclassman was one of the finest that was ever seen in the state of Maryland. We were undefeated in our division and went on to win the state championship. Many of the senior players received All-Metropolitan honors and full scholarships to large state universities. My superior, the gentleman who was the first-string fullback, was the captain of the team. He was also the president of the senior class and a straight-A student, as near an example of the Renaissance Jock as ever carried the pigskin. The senior fullback was so valiant, gifted and tireless that, despite a trick knee, which continually pained him, he rarely left the game. So I rode the bench most of the first year.

It was also to be my last year of football. I had finally gotten inside the game, and what I saw there was strange; try as I would I could not adapt to it. What to me had been great fun, feeling the exhilaration of my own power over others, suddenly had become deadly serious. The heroes of the Northwestern football team were not playing a game. They wanted desperately to kill somebody.

If you have not played organized football on the high school or college level you cannot imagine what goes on in the locker room before a game. In the sixties we called it getting "psyched up," and the term is so apt that I suppose it hasn't changed. The ritual began several minutes before the game, when the field lights were blazing and we could hear the roar of the crowd awaiting our entrance. It was ostensibly to settle our equipment, the complex of shoulder pads, hip guards, etc. You would face a teammate your own size, and as if shaking hands, grab his right elbow with your right hand, as he held your right elbow with his right hand. And you would both pull with all your might, slamming your right shoulder against his, once, twice, again and again until you could hear your teeth rattle. Then with the left shoulder, wham, wham until a kind of giddiness ensued, a semi-consciousness in which you could hear savage, bloodthirsty cries, epithets and execrations not permitted in the lowest circles of hell. And then you would slam your partner with both hands against his shoulders, so maybe he would crash into the locker behind him, and he would return the favor. Then, hand in hand, you would bang your helmets together like gongs screaming, "Are you psyched, are you *psyched*? We gonna kill the some bitches?"

I could not get psyched. My soul would slip out of my body and perch on top of one of the lockers watching this ritual in amusement, and then horror. The soul of a true football player does not go wandering around the locker room commenting on the body's behavior. It is a contemptible failure of concentration. This failure of concentration was duly noticed by my teammates, who continued to treat me with professional courtesy, but some restraint, which may have been the beginnings of suspicion.

During the summer tryouts my senior year I remember overhearing a conversation about myself, which was only half finished as I was entering the locker room. I heard something like: "Well, he *looks* like a football player, at least—" and then an awkward silence as I walked into their space. As the summer wore on and the heat died, and the leaves began falling, I was beginning to dread the long twilights of football practice, the constant pounding, the soreness (which has never left me to this day), the mindless driving of the blocking sleds uphill with bruised shoulders, like a slave. And my time had come. I had inherited the responsibilities of the senior fullback. No more riding the bench—a season of warfare stretched before me.

After a grueling practice the week before our first game, we were all sitting on the fifty-yard line listening to a lecture on aggression. My mind was a thousand miles away. Over the summer I had toured the capitals of Europe instead of training for football. I was seventeen years old, and a little slower off the blocks than I had been the year before. I was in love, which is no common incentive to murder. I had begun to write poems and fill out applications to small liberal arts colleges where I would study literature, and philosophy, and never look at another football.

At the end of practice I told the coach I would be turning in my uniform. Dan Palumbo was fifty-five years old and had been coaching for thirty years. Half Sicilian, half American Indian, Palumbo was hard as a baseball bat. He looked like the chief on the old buffalo nickel. When he smiled, which was infrequent, his face would crack into a million tiny lines and his eyes would light up, while his mouth remained curled downward. Now he was not smiling. He knew I was struggling and was probably relieved at the chance to wash his hands of me, as if I had been some truly vile substance. Now he could not look at me. He was sneering, and shaking his head. The only words he uttered were: "You're too slow, kid. You're too slow." I had never been particularly fast for a backfield man. What I lacked in speed I more than made up for in determination, the desire to make the team, the desire to prove my strength, and nerve; but my desire had shifted toward more mysterious and intangible goals.

The Violin Lesson

My friend Daniel Heifetz can stand on the stage with a violin pressed between his cheek and shoulder, and make thousands of people weep and tremble. I have seen him do this. And it seemed to me, a devoted amateur, that little cherubs with halos fluttered around the head of his fiddle. I would be envious if I did not know how hard he works to keep those cherubs under control. He does this year in and year out and his career as a concert musician takes him to Los Angeles, Munich, Singapore and the ends of the earth. At home, when he is not practicing, or looking after his children, Heifetz teaches young violinists from the Peabody Conservatory. Father, husband, artist and teacher, Daniel Heifetz is a young man with exacting responsibilities.

Not the least of Heifetz's concerns is his violin, which is two hundred and sixty-three years old, approximately two hundred and twenty-seven years older than either of us. It even has a name. His violin is called the DeChaponay Stradivarius, after a French count who owned it until his death in 1877. I have seen the DeChaponay listed in the classic study of Stradivari's life and work, written by Hill, Hill and Hill and published in 1902. In that faraway time the Hill brothers were calling the DeChaponay one of the finest instruments made in the year 1722, when the violin maker was in his ultimate maturity as a craftsman.

Now there is little doubt that the violins made by Antonio Stradivari in the late seventeenth and early eighteenth centuries are the finest ever heard. Since only several hundred still exist, the best ones are priceless, though money does change hands when a Strad passes from one owner to another. A great deal of money. Not to mince words, my friend's violin is one of the most valuable pieces of wood in the world, and has been famous for at least a century. The DeChaponay has an armored case that would survive fire, flood and artillery shells. The first time I visited the Heifetz household I became aware of more than the usual clicking and clacking of locks, and beeping of burglar alarms on crossing the threshold. I wondered aloud if my friend did not have an excessive fear of thieves, and he replied, smiling: "It's for the violin." The annual insurance premium on the DeChaponay Stradivarius would suffice to pay a child's private school tuition for two years. Without the alarm system the premium would be even higher.

This responsibility which my friend bears with pride and equanimity seems totally overwhelming to me. So one day over lunch, when our conversation turned to the pressures of adulthood, Heifetz mentioned his violin, and I could not contain myself. Half joking, I suggested that he sell it.

"Sell my fiddle?" The violinist looked at me at first in disbelief, as if he had not heard me correctly, and then with some indulgence, as if I had been one of his children.

But I went on. "Sure," I said. "You own it, don't you?"

He nodded. "Well—" he sighed,—"I do have a copy of it that I practice on, now and then."

"How does it sound?"

"Oh, it sounds very good! It was made by one of the

greatest living craftsmen, and it's a perfect copy of the DeChaponay."

"So just how much better is the Stradivarius?" I demanded. "I mean, if there's not all *that* much difference, wouldn't it be a load off your mind to sell the Stradivarius and perform on the copy?"

By then my friend's amusement had reached such a pitch that he became animated about the question. He began to play along. He began to advance the reputation of the modern copy crafted by Peter Paul Prier in Salt Lake City. Heifetz attested that the Prier violin had a truly noble presence and an eloquent tone. In a practice room one could hardly distinguish between the sound of the Stradivarius and its copy—if anything, the DeChaponay sounded less comfortable, like a large man in a small room.

In fact Heifetz had such confidence in the Prier violin that he was lending it to his prize student for her debut with the Baltimore Symphony. The student, Wanchi Huang, traveled from Taiwan two years ago to study with Heifetz. Now she had earned her place on the program of a major symphony orchestra by winning a statewide competition for high school musicians. Her own violin, machine-made, was more than adequate for the practice room, but unequal to the occasion of her debut, which was to be that very evening.

"Would you like to come?" he asked. "You can give me support, because I will be more nervous than my student. And you will get to hear a good performance on the Prier violin, so you can better advise me about keeping the Stradivarius."

I agreed to go along.

The symphony hall was full as our young soloist entered,

violin in hand, amid thundering applause, as if the audience would do all it could to frighten her. Demure yet poised in her dress of pink tulle, Wanchi Huang smiled, bowed professionally and answered the baton of the conductor.

She played the Introduction and Rondo Capriccioso of Saint-Saëns, a virtuoso piece. Written for the violinist Pablo de Sarasate, the music has a distinct Spanish flavor. The langorous excitement of the first melody gives way to a lively rondo with runs and smooth singing phrases, staccato passages like castanetes, unexpected leaps and plunges, and colorful double-stopping. Wanchi performed with extraordinary self-possession for a fifteen-year-old. She was in command throughout and at no point did the Prier violin let her down: it sang warmly, exactly, with sensitivity to her moods. The ending of the Capriccioso is a desperate, breathless race to the finish, and the Prier delivered every note perfectly, without blurring or discoloration.

The applause doubled that which had welcomed her. Wanchi's teacher was smiling broadly and told me, above the clamor, that she had played beautifully, far better before the crowd than in private, which is one sign of a great future. I thanked him for inviting me to hear her.

Later in the evening, after the reception for Wanchi, Heifetz asked me what I had thought of the Prier violin. I told him that although there were no other violins that night playing the Saint-Saëns, I felt sure no instrument could pay a more eloquent tribute to the work. Frowning, Heifetz agreed, adding, however, that he had never had the privilege of sitting in the audience while he *himself* stood on the stage and played. In fact he had never heard himself playing the Stradivarius *or* the Prier at any creditable distance. I told him I understood the problem.

Though we could not solve that problem we did the next best thing. Two days later we packed up the violins, called Wanchi, who agreed to come along, and headed for the empty concert hall. We had Wanchi's machine-made instrument. We had Heifetz's copy of the DeChaponay, made by Peter Paul Prier. And then we had the DeChaponay Stradivarius itself, sleeping in its bulletproof coffin like Dracula. Heifetz and I stood in the middle of the auditorium while Wanchi stood on the stage, surrounded by fiddles, music stands and forlorn harps and pianos. She would begin with the younger violins.

Wanchi played the Introduction of the Saint-Saëns as she had the night of her debut, but on the machine-made violin the sound was smaller. Some of the notes got lost altogether, and the ones that did reach us lacked body. As we moved closer to the stage we could hear more, but the tone did not improve. All the notes were there, and extremely accurate, since this was Wanchi's familiar instrument.

"Thank you," called Heifetz. "Now play the same on the Prier."

The difference was remarkable. It could be described most definitely as a difference of size—with the same apparent effort the violinist delivered notes that were louder and of slightly more duration than before. It was as if some aperture through which the sound must pass had been widened. The melancholy Introduction to the Rondo, which on the machine-made violin sounded rather like a whimper, now sounded like a full-blown complaint that could not be ignored. We had been listening through a keyhole, and now the Prier had opened the door.

"Wanchi," called Heifetz. He had to call her twice. "Now play it on the Strad."

As she lifted the DeChaponay carefully from the velvet lining of its case, I thought I could hear it groan, like someone who is unaccustomed to being disturbed for trifles. The Stradivarius is several shades darker than the Prier, but otherwise looks the same. With some difficulty of adjustment which I did not understand, a faint rasping in the strings, Wanchi started once more upon the Saint-Saëns Introduction. The sound was noticeably larger than the Prier's though the difference was not dramatic or to the discredit of the younger violin. But there was something else.

Heifetz looked at me with some intensity.

"Do you hear it?" my friend asked. And I admitted that I could indeed, as anyone with ears would have to admit that he heard thunder. But I did not know if I could tell him what, exactly, I was hearing, or how much it was influenced by myth. After all, an amateur is only an amateur, no matter how passionate, and it suddenly occurred to me that I might be deaf compared to Heifetz. As first I perceived the difference as a greater fullness, a kind of "booming" in the lower register. Then I observed that during the rests, the notes simply lasted longer than the Prier's while never stumbling over one another or blurring in the trills.

Heifetz had not invited me there to entertain me. He wanted me to tell him what I was hearing, honestly and without embellishment, as if the violins had been on trial for some serious offense. The teacher thanked his student, and took her place on the stage. Now I was on trial as well, for although Heifetz might listen to Wanchi play the violins, he could not listen to himself. And that would have been the only true test, for him. The Stradivarius, unlike the Guarneri and Amati, is not an accommodating instrument. The Stradivarius "resists" the performer and the music has to be coaxed from it. Great musicians learn how to harness this energy, but it takes long practice and familiarity with the particular violin. No one, at present, can put the DeChaponay through its paces but Daniel Heifetz. And he had invited me to judge its performance, a task that humbled me. If I could describe the violin's distinction, then it must be very obvious indeed.

In Heifetz's hands the machine-made violin actually sounded worse than before, though it was hard to tell whether it was suffering now by comparison with the finer instruments, or at the hands of a stranger. He was clearly struggling to get the best notes out of Wanchi's violin, but some got lost and others seemed to fuse, particularly in the arpeggios and trills. Heifetz set the fiddle down, and took up the honey-colored Prier.

After a few strokes of adjustment Heifetz began playing the Bruch concerto, and we perceived a tone that was clearly superior to anything we had yet heard. The first movement of that piece, slow, mysterious though linear, is a test of range from low to high tones. For the first time the hall was full of music. Each note, round and precise, seemed to reach the ceiling and the far corners of the space. That is what I told him when he called to me, and later I admitted I did not know if it were the violin or his playing that made it so. Then he played some of the Tchaikovsky concerto, to test the high notes, which were clear and ringing. To display the violin's brilliance in arpeggiation he began the Bach Chaconne, and it was so beautiful I begged him not to stop.

But Heifetz had not come to play me a concert. He set down the Prier copy of the DeChaponay, and picked up the thing itself. Now as Heifetz raised the Stradivarius to his shoulder his eyes drooped slightly, while losing none of their alertness. A visible peace descended upon him, a sunny hypnotic calm which communicated itself to the entire hall, to Wanchi and myself. I remembered the last time I had seen him play the same calm descended upon several thousand people. Whether the musician made that happen, or the DeChaponay had made its uncanny power visible through him, even in silence, no one will ever know.

Suddenly a high note cut through the air, dividing the auditorium like a lightning bolt. It was the high note of the famous opening of Beethoven's concerto for violin and orchestra, wherein the violin seems to be climbing up the side of a mountain from which it has been promised a view of paradise. I said that the note came like lightning, yet it hung in the air like a star.

I am not making poetry, for it would serve neither my purpose nor the violinist's. The fact is, there are few ways of describing differences of tonal quality. It is not enough to say that the DeChaponay has more volume than the other violins, or that its notes have more duration and resonance. As Heifetz played that high note of the Beethoven, working up to it again, and again, I realized that the note, like any star or light source, had an aura, which faded as it receded from the brilliance of its center. That was the "edge" of the sound, the split second when it becomes silence. The notes of the other violins, however brilliant at the center, sometimes wavered uneasily at the edge of silence, like a child afraid of diving off a cliff. The edge of the DeChaponay's note, on the other hand, rainbowed into the silence with perfect consistency and grace.

Heifetz moved from the dramatic opening of the Beethoven concerto to its tragic cadenza, wherein the violin sings a duet with itself, high and low. And suddenly there were the cherubs, I could see them cavorting around the violin head. Considering the intricate braiding of the many sounds, each with its own aura, it seemed incredible to me that none of the colors was lost, and that the DeChaponay, in Heifetz's hands, could keep all of those sounds in balance.

"Well," he called. "What do you think?"

I looked at Wanchi, who was grinning, but professionally cool all the same. I had a lot of thoughts, so many I did not know where to begin. I wanted to call out that the thing was alive, that Antonio Stradivari had endowed the raw maplewood with his wisdom, which was the sum of what the Western world had learned about music as of 1722; that since then the violin had absorbed the intelligence of every violinist who played it, as well as the emotion of countless wars, deaths, births and marriages which it had outlived. And like any sagacious creature the DeChaponay had used experience to its advantage. I wanted to tell him the violin had frightening power, not only to express his musical genius, but to influence it.

I can say without embarrassment that I did not know what to tell Heifetz without sounding like a fool or madman. And by now I had the feeling that I could not tell him much he did not already know.

So I kept it short. "It is like you are playing an instrument that is a foot longer than the others. The music goes farther, and lasts longer because it seems to come from a deeper source. I don't know."

"What do you mean you don't know?" he replied, laughing.

Again Heifetz took up the Bach Chaconne, a piece for solo violin that displays the most ingenious and soul-searching arpeggiation. The cherubs began dancing around the peg scrolls, and a few demons joined them. The DeChaponay was scattering light all over the symphony hall, like a diamond. Wanchi confessed her admiration, while admitting a professional loyalty to the younger instruments, which were far more comfortable.

Later my friend asked me, with a charming air of innocence, if he should keep his Stradivarius. Wanting him to know just how well I had learned my lesson, I told him he should find the DeChaponay's twin, and lock one in a vault, in case something should happen to the other.

As a writer, I am glad there are no pens like that.

Passover Night and
Easter Morning

S pringtime came flowering with the golden forsythia, the eager hyacinth and crocus, then the mockingbird singing in the pale willow. And for one boy of twelve, spring came upon a wind of promise and grave responsibility. Two challenges faced me, each unrivaled in all the months of summer, fall and winter combined, two tests of my ability and courage. First, I would preside over the sacred rituals of the Passover Seder, the Jewish feast of thanksgiving for deliverance from Egypt. Then, two days later, I would sing a solo in the Easter choir.

My Jewish father had married a Christian, an event no one on either side of the family could explain or wholly forgive. Here is the way the story was told to me: My father heard of my mother's beauty and drove a hundred miles from the city to verify it. He liked what he saw, returned once, twice, to take the small-town beauty on long drives in the country, while neighbors gossiped about the swarthy invader and my mother's sister barred the door. The third time out my mother told him to keep right on driving, through Maryland, Virginia, and into North Carolina. Had she been an Arab, or he a Montague and she a Capulet, he would not have turned around. They had some regard for their virtue, if none for religion, and stopped somewhere long enough to find a justice of the peace, who heard their vows.

When I was born, a year later, it was time to consider how

to raise the child—as a Christian or as a Jew. My parents decided I should be both. Such a wealth of wisdom and culture in Judaism *and* Christianity! It must have seemed somehow ungrateful, or wasteful, to choose between the two. So my mother and father presented this decision, or indecision, to the family at large, who had little choice but to live with it. And live with it they did, each side of the family educating me in its own beliefs as far as it might without showing disrespect for the other.

That is how I came to sing my solo in the Easter choir. My mother's mother, as upright and refined an Episcopalian lady as ever fried a rockfish or hoed beets, was a pillar of the church. She was *the* pillar, to be exact, for the clapboard sanctuary with its one-belled steeple could scarcely have used more than one pillar and a few corner beams and still made room for the dozen pews and the pedal organ. I doubt my grandmother had ever laid eyes on a Jew before she saw my father. When, suddenly, she found she had a grandson who was half-Jewish, she did what any sensible Episcopalian lady would have done. She put me to work in the church.

My grandfather, a cheerful, silver-haired Dutchman, was the sexton. Sunday mornings he would take me with him to church early to light the kerosene stove and ring the bell. I could just reach the knot of the bell rope. Pulling with all my weight, I could hear it clang, and then I would hold on as the heavy bell, returning in its arc above, yanked the rope, and me hanging from it, high over the pews and my laughing grandfather. He shared my grandmother's commitment to the church, but not her piety. He was in it for the music.

Singing was the second great love of my grandfather's life, the first being my grandmother. When my grandfather was fifteen, on shore leave for the first time in America, he paid a month's sea wages to stand at the back of the Metropolitan Opera House and hear Caruso. Forty years later, he would weep recalling the genius of the incomparable tenor, singing me passages of *La Traviata* as illustrations, in an accent that was neither Italian nor Dutch.

So for my grandfather, the church was a place to sing, listen to someone sing, or be heard singing. From the beginning of time, it seemed, my grandfather had sung the offertory solo on Easter morning. That tradition was as constant as the lilies on the altar and the sunshine on the purple hyacinths in the churchyard. It never rained on Easter. The sun shone, fresh from its winter's rest, pouring through the stained-glass windows on my grandfather's white surplice and whiter hair as the organ bellowed and he rose to sing "O see the place where Jesus lay. . . ."

He always had a fine natural tenor. But on Easter my grandfather surpassed himself, singing as he always dreamed he might sing. Folks in the Methodist church across the street would sneak out to listen outside our door. Tramps who had no church of their own would wander in and stand in the aisle as if under hypnosis. Each spring my grandfather's solo improved, despite his age and failing health. When he rose to sing, the years would fall from him like a thin disguise for the perennial, indomitable voice. In the last years he generated such emotion that no one in the family could bear it, and during his solo they would leave the church to make room for the strangers who had come from miles around to hear him sing.

So the year my grandfather decided that I should sing the solo on Easter morning, I was flabbergasted, and flattered, and terrified. For one thing, my voice was changing: cracking, and yodeling and hiding at the most inopportune moments. My grandfather paid no attention, assuming, I suppose, that whatever genius had inspired him every Easter for thirty years would pass to his grandson along with the assignment. This was his idea of immortality.

At the time, I had another thing on my mind. In the autumn I would be Bar Mitzvahed. This is the ceremonial confirmation of Jewish manhood, the day one joins the elders in reading from the Torah. My friends in Hebrew school already teased me about having a mother who was not Jewish, though that was clearly no fault of mine. But if they heard I had been singing in a *choir!* On *Easter!* They would think I was totally crazy, *meshugga*, and I would never hear the end of it.

The nearness of my Bar Mitzvah encouraged my father to put me in charge of the Passover supper. Those who celebrate the deliverance from Egypt in their own homes know that the family patriarch or head of the household presides over the beautiful rituals of the Passover Seder. The idea of my father's leaving the task to his twelve-year-old son may seem strange. But there was nobody else alive who knew the role.

I was the first child in two generations who was not either too poor or too busy to go to Hebrew school. My father's grandparents were Orthodox Jews from Russia. When my father was a boy, he celebrated Passover in their home, where the rituals were carried on as they were in the old country, as a way of life. Then there was a lost generation. My father's father and uncles and aunts were all born in America during hard times, before World War I. Staying alive was a full-time job for those immigrants and their children, who sold papers and shined shoes and worked in their parents' grocery. There was little time for studying. Poverty did not relax its hold on our family until the 1950s, when my father paid his debts. And the very next thing he did was send his son to Hebrew school.

Since the death of my great-grandparents, the Passover Seder had been a strange festival indeed, with gorgeous props and symbols whose importance no one doubted and whose meaning no one understood. My Great-aunt Jule set her table for the feast as she had done for fifty years, first under the eagle eye of her Orthodox mother, and then on her own, as if she were still being watched. On the long, immaculate white tablecloth lay the ritual plates. A white napkin covered one plate with three sheets of matzo, the unleavened bread. Another plate held a weird zodiac of objects clearly meant more for contemplation than digestion: a charred shank bone, a horseradish sliced and ground, a sprig of parsley, a concoction of chopped apples and nuts and wine called *charoseth*, and a boiled egg. There was one bowl filled with salt water, and another with fresh. There were bed pillows with embroidered cases on every chair. And there was a magnum of red wine and a silver goblet filled for the prophet Elijah, for whom the door would be opened so he might sip, invisibly, from the gleaming brim.

If those dinner arrangements would not drive a child mad with curiosity and suspense, neither would all the tales of the Arabian nights. By the time I had learned the famous Four Questions in Hebrew school, I had asked them all a hundred times in English and had made up some of my own: Why is this night different from all other nights? Why are we eating this hard crumbly matzo instead of real bread? Why do I have to eat that bitter horseradish that stings my tongue? Why are we dipping our celery into the bowl of water? And what are those pillows doing on the chairs—are we going to sleep here? There was not a soul in the house who could answer me. They had to send me to Hebrew school so I could learn the answers for all of them.

So that year, the same year my Dutch grandfather chose for me to sing the solo in the Easter choir, I was planning my first Passover Seder. It was a busy time. When I was not singing scales, I was studying the *Haggadah*, a wonderful book about Moses and the Exodus that is also the script for the Passover supper. If my father's family had not had a proper Seder in twenty years, they deserved the best. I would not let them down. By mid-April I was fit to direct anybody's Seder, in English or Hebrew. I could almost feel the long beard spilling into my lap, the badge of piety and erudition.

I had forgotten one thing: their appetite. All those years of religious neglect had coincided with a great hunger, and so my relatives had come to invest all their emotional energy in the one part of the symbolism they understood: the food. They arrived sniffing the aroma of roast chicken and beef brisket and my Aunt Jule's prize chopped liver, and they were hardly out of their hats and coats before they were into the dinning room nibbling from the sideboard. Jule announced, "This year the boy will do the *baruchas*, like in the old days!" Everyone nodded and beamed at me as my slender Aunt Jean pinched my cheek. My mustachioed Uncle Arthur and the soft-spoken Uncle Leonard took turns wringing my hand and slapping me on the back. Then my Aunt Jule called us to the table.

I raised the first cup of wine under the proud gaze of all my relatives. I blessed the wine, in Hebrew, and a great cheer went up before they drained their glasses. "Not too bad,"

said my Uncle Leonard. "Not too bad for a mere *boychik.*" I
called for the plate of herbs, dipped a slice of spring onion
into the salt water, and passed it to Uncle Arthur on my left
as I blessed the fruit of the earth. Then I felt for the middle
matzo on the napkin-covered dish, broke it in two, and
asked my Aunt Helen to hide half of it.

"Hide it?" asked Uncle Arthur, smoothing his mustache.
"Who from? Who would steal it? When are we going to eat,
anyway?"

My patient Aunt Helen recalled that this was part of the
ceremony, that whoever found the hidden matzo got a prize.

"Do they get fed?" asked Uncle Leonard.

I withered him with my gaze.

Then I uncovered the matzo, lifted the plate, and said, "Lo!
This is the bread of affliction which our ancestors ate in the
land of Egypt. Let all who are hungry eat thereof. . . ."

"Now," said Uncle Arthur, striking the board with a fist,
"now we're getting someplace." He went for the matzo,
which I held just beyond his reach.

I continued, "Let all who are in need come and celebrate
the Passover." I asked my father to open the front door for
Elijah, and said, "As our door is open, may not only the hungry come but also the spirit of the prophet of Elijah, that we
may tonight think wisely and feel deeply as we celebrate the
Passover." And I poured the silver goblet full for Elijah,
singing, "Elijah the prophet, Elijah the Tishbite, Elijah the
Gileadite. . . ."

"Who wound *him* up?" my Uncle Leonard whispered to
Aunt Helen, as I launched into the Four Questions, in my
best Hebrew singing voice. I knew I was in trouble when my
aunts' smiles began to sag, and then Aunt Jean fell asleep. Yet
I would not be daunted. I was full of the glory of my enter-

prise, being the first Seder director ever to both ask and answer the Four Questions, a one-man yeshiva. They would have to drag me away.

The company was in sullen revolt. Uncle Arthur had escaped into the kitchen. Another two or three aunts were dozing, apparently bloodless from hunger. My patient father had advanced to the fourth cup of wine and was pouring a fifth for Uncle Leonard. By the time I rolled up to my favorite part of the ceremony, reciting the plagues upon the Egyptians—Frogs, Vermin, Pestilence, Locusts—while flinging bloodlike drops of wine upon the white plate, I was a desperate man. It was clear there was but one plague that mattered to my relatives: this precocious, inexhaustible twelve-year-old. . . I was more terrible than the Pharoah.

"Enough already," said my Aunt Jule. "The meat will be dry." Suddenly everybody woke up. They were cheering me and slapping me on the back again as my aunts entered, shouldering tureens of matzoball soup and gefilte fish, and beef brisket and chicken.

"What about the *Dayenu*?" I wailed. "What about the bitter herbs and the *charoseth*?"

"Next year," said Uncle Leonard kindly, patting my hand as he gulped soup. "You can begin where you left off."

Now that the food was on the table, their appreciation knew no bounds. "The boy did a great job, didn't he?" asked Uncle Arthur, passing me the chopped liver. "Eat," he said, "you earned it."

"Mamma would have been proud," said my blond Aunt Billie, misting up a little.

"And Papa," added my Aunt Jean.

"And *Henry*," said my father. "Henry would have *loved* it," said my aunts, in chorus.

My Aunt Jule raised her wineglass. "To Henry," she proclaimed, and the entire family drank to the memory of Uncle Henry.

My father's Uncle Henry, recently deceased, had paid for my aunt's house and lived there in his last years. He had carried the whole family on his shoulders through the Depression and World War II. With no education, he took what work he could get. In the 1920s, he worked for Al Capone in the wine and spirits business. Later, Henry owned his own liquor business and branched out into the games-of-chance business. Everybody in the family worked for him who was able, and those who were not able remained on the payroll. He was handsome and charming, with a boxer's physique, and he combed his hair straight back from his forehead like George Raft. His shoes were always shiny. My Uncle Henry valued a sense of humor above all things. Uncertain of how to communicate this to a child, he used to buy me handshake buzzers and whoopee cushions and exploding cigarettes, and urge me to try them on our relatives. If they didn't laugh when the cigarette exploded, then we would have nothing more to do with them.

Henry's sense of humor extended to the marriage between my father and my Christian mother. He loved my mother deeply. When no one else in my father's family would have much to do with her, Henry treated my mother like a daughter. He would take her side in any conflict with my father, which was helpful, because my father also worked for Henry and idolized him. When money was tight and my mother begged for a piano, it was Henry who saw to it she got her piano. He was the one person in the family with whom no one disagreed.

So my aunt's house was full of Uncle Henry. The bedroom upstairs where I slept on Passover night was a shrine to his memory: photographs of Henry with Jule, with the mayor and governor; old suits in the closet and a rusted revolver in the drawer of the nightstand. If there was an invisible guest on Passover, who blew in when we opened the door and sipped from the silver brim of Elijah's cup, it was my father's Uncle Henry.

Full of the excitement of my Seder triumph, I lay on my uncle's bed, wide-eyed, for a long time, worrying about Easter. How could I sing that solo? I mean, after Exodus and the Forty Years in the desert, after all my years in Hebrew school and hours of studying the *Haggadah*, how could I stand up in a church on the holiest Christian holiday and sing for them? But then, how could I not? My grandfather would be heartbroken.

If it had not been for the four glasses of wine I drank when I was supposed to be sipping, I might never have slept. As it was, the sleep that finally came was fitful and streaked with dreams that were like waking in a world where thoughts are as vivid as furniture. Long about midnight, I heard a scuffling in the closet.

The door creaked open, and somebody was standing at the foot of my bed. A single ray of street light from the window fell full upon his face. It was Uncle Henry. He looked okay.

"Hello, kid," said Henry.

"Uncle Henry!" I said. "Is this some kind of a practical joke?"

Henry laughed. "I always said you had a great sense of humor. Remember when we put the rubber scorpion in Aunt Jule's martini? No, all jokes aside, I came to check up on you.

Like I said, I always knew you had a sense of humor, but I never knew you would be such a scholar. That was a great show you put on tonight."

"You were there?"

"Wouldn't have missed it for the world. I was real proud."

"Thanks, Uncle Henry." I was embarrassed, thinking about what I was going to do on Sunday. I was not going to tell him, but he knew anyway. One problem with dead people is that you cannot keep any secrets from them.

"So *nu*?" said Henry. "What's the trouble?"

"The solo. My grandfather wants me to sing the solo on Easter Sunday. I don't know if I can go through with it."

"So let's hear it," said Henry. He sat in a Morris chair next to the window, his shoes shining in the street light. Uncle Henry was not the sort of man who would take no for an answer. I sang the song.

"That was terrific," said Henry. "I would clap, but you wouldn't hear anything. You sing real good, except every now and then on a high note your voice cracks. But, hey, you're only young once. You'll be fine."

"You mean you think it's all right?" I asked. "The words and all? On Easter?"

"Why not?" Henry shrugged. "It's music, kid, it's all music. You know, I never met your mother's father, but I always heard he has a great sense of humor. You can't let him down. And then, what about all those people in church? Are you going to deny them the pleasure of your singing because you are a Jew?"

"But do I have to sing about Jesus?"

"Listen to me, kid, and listen good. You are a guest in their joint, and you sing what *they* want you to sing. When they come to the synagogue, then we'll make them sing the *shema*. If there was one thing Jesus understood, it was tolerance."

I did not want to argue with Uncle Henry, him being dead and all.

"Now you better get some sleep," he said, and he was gone.

On Easter morning the little church was full of the fragrance of lilies. Ladies sat with their white-gloved hands in their laps, beaming under broad and beribboned hats next to men craning their necks from stiff collars and hushing the fidgeting children. I rose from my seat in the choir at the summons of the organ. My grandfather, on my right, squeezed my arm, and my mother nodded encouragement. Only one of my Jewish relatives had made it to the Easter service, and I was the only person who knew he was there. As I began to sing, the church door blew open, filling the aisle with light.

Thanksgiving Grace

The drive to my grandmother's house on Thanksgiving morning was like a journey back in time. It was Indian summer, autumn's last stand against the cold. Under a clear sky my mother and I were returning from winter to autumn as we traveled southeast of the city. Bare branches and violet shades of November fell behind us. Along the roadside through fields of burnt-out corn and tobacco the yellow leaves clung to the oaks, and the goldenrod glowed under red maples.

And it seemed we were going back much further than a season. The town where my mother grew up had not grown up with her. The shuttered, clapboard houses with their screened porches looked both frail and immortal behind the giant sycamores and pecan trees that might never grow or die. There were no new houses. The same hundred ladies in their black hats and white gloves poured out of the houses on Sunday and into the four churches to pray, presumably, for God's grace in maintaining a world that could not be improved by change. My mother's home town was the perfect preservative of holiday customs, and we could be sure to find there a Thanksgiving worthy of any Pilgrim.

I could not think of Thanksgiving without Pilgrims. Pilgrims and Indians. My schoolbook showed their pictures. Pilgrims in their conical black hats with circular brims shading their eyes, Pilgrims with shiny buckles and blunderbusses at their sides, serious Pilgrims gathered together around a table of rough-hewn boards. And in the foreground a procession of kindly Indians, bronze skinned, relaxed; some standing, some kneeling, one bowing. The brave and gentle Indians came bearing the fruits of the season: oaken bowls of berries, figs and wild asparagus, trenchers of deer meat, turkey and rabbit, sweetcorn and clay pots of steaming, mysterious soup.

The Pilgrims looked prim yet grateful. The Indians looked dignified and reserved despite their nakedness and generosity. Those Indians were the perfect instruments of grace. In a fantasy I mixed this picture with my memory of the cornucopia, the horn of plenty with all the world's food cascading out of it. I saw a painted, dignified Indian standing at the head of the Pilgrims' table, holding the cornucopia which spilled a colorful stream of bounty into the plates of the Pilgrims, who looked grateful, at the same time they appeared too refined ever to *eat* anything.

I was starving. My mother, one hand on the steering wheel, the other rummaging in the picnic basket, offered me an egg, a carrot spear, an oatmeal cookie. I waved them away, staring out at the saltmarsh on the horizon. I would not eat. I was twelve years old and one of the first boys of the second generation to test their appetites against my grand-mother's Thanksgiving dinner. I had not eaten since the night before. I was creating a vacuum within me to accommodate the hopes of my uncles, aunts, grandparents and cousins. If I did not eat, eat vastly and zealously and for a long time, what comment would I be making upon my grandmother's Art, what anticlimax would I be serving History itself!

So I nursed my hunger, feeling its edge like the point of a

weapon, as our car crunched into the gravel of my grandparents' driveway. We were surrounded by aunts and uncles, and little cousins pressing their noses against the windshield. My mother's sister pulled my mother from the car to hug her. They look alike except that my aunt is darker and taller and seems stern from school teaching; but though my mother is always first to start them laughing, my aunt is the last to stop. My button-nosed cousin David, who feared the moon, pressed a football to my chest and "went deep" beyond the garden for me to throw it to him while another boy chased him, little Glen, so nearsighted he might run into the japonica bush. My grandfather, beaming at the sight of my mother, strolled from the garage, where the gentlemen snuck whiskey. My flaxen-haired cousin Marie, my own age, stood by the kitchen door looking at her feet. We had reached the age when our passions ran so high we could scarcely speak to each other.

The house was ringing with laughter of ladies in the parlor sipping muscatel, and children racing down and upstairs and through the bedrooms slamming doors. My grandmother in the kitchen, a delicate glass of sherry on the sideboard at her elbow, was the eye of the storm. Surrounded by bubbling, steaming, roasting and effervescent food, she tolerated the daughters and nieces who begged to serve her, but needed no help. She needed only God's help and seemed to have plenty of it. She set down a huge wooden spoon, wiped her long hands on her flowerprint apron, and gave me a hug that smelled of rosemary.

My grandmother was the Queen of Thanksgiving. She was an Indian and she was a Pilgrim, being both an instrument of grace and a beneficiary of it. Stirring the fragrant gravy, she intoned a hymn. My grandmother had been a striking young woman, tall, chestnut-haired, with high cheekbones her daughters had inherited. She was half Cherokee Indian. Her nose was so finely shaped that when time turned it slightly to the side it looked like she had been walking boldly into the wind. She became a beautiful old woman despite the trials and tragedies of motherhood, the strain of the Depression, cooking and housekeeping without machines or servants. Her eldest daughter said the woman did nothing but work, and sleep, and pray.

She was the most grateful of women. My grandmother was grateful for her health and her children's health, for her strength and beauty, for the roof over her head and the food on her table. She was aware that many envied her lot, and so labored to be worthy of that grace. Thanksgiving was her chance to provide an edible display of her invisible gratitude. All that the rest of us could do, in humble response, was to stuff ourselves just shy of bursting.

The eating contest had commenced during the Great Depression. My grandmother cooked then for her husband and three children, as well as for her sister and the seven sons of her sister, whose husband had succumbed to a frail liver. The boys were hungry. They woke up hungry, and the ladle of grits for breakfast only teased their appetites. In the summer they gathered blackberries, and caught shad and smoked it on the riverbank. They raided the fields for tomatoes, corn and peas. The boys went to bed hungry, talking to their innards. In October they filched apples and pears. But it seemed that whatever they ate only made their appetites grow faster than their arms and legs.

So when Thanksgiving came my grandfather did whatever he had to do to make sure there would be more food on the table than twenty lumberjacks could consume. Growing up in Holland during World War I, my grandfather had survived a blockade when the starving Dutch were driven to eat the poisonous tulip bulbs. My grandfather was concerned that the boys get enough to eat all year 'round, but on Thanksgiving they should have such an abundance they might forget their hunger at least for a day or two. In the presence of so much turkey and ham and cornbread the boys quickly overcame their humility, and grew bold. Soon as they had conquered their hunger they turned to challenge each other's capacity.

Those were the immemorial titans, the mythic eaters of Thanksgiving dinner. Something of the excitement was lost by the second generation. We could not match the hunger or the heroic capacity of the Depression eaters. It was a matter of family record and the stuff of legends that in 1937 my cousin Marvin so covered himself with glory at the Thanksgiving feast, he became the wonder and despair of all who followed him. There were other stories of Marvin, the child genius, who built radios from tin cans and once distinguished himself by affixing a plumber's plunger to his right ear. But on that Thanksgiving day that would live forever in the family memory, my experimental cousin Marvin put himself outside an entire turkey, fully stuffed, at a sitting.

There had been many stout turkeys in 1937, scaled down from twenty-five to eighteen pounds. One of the birds was assigned to Marvin at his request. The other boys would compete against each other, dismembering the larger fowl. But Marvin was in a class by himself—it was Marvin against the lone turkey. Napkin bibbed under his broad chin, fisted knife and fork aiming at the ceiling while my grandfather said grace, Marvin glowered at the complacent turkey stretched with chestnut stuffing, garnished with parsley and glazed carrots.

"Marvin," sneered his lean brother, Luther. "You aren't going to eat that *whole* turkey."

Marvin looked at his brother as if he were a doorstop. "Pass me those mashed potatoes, Luther," said Marvin. Luther complied. Marvin heaped his plate with the buttery potatoes, and with the same shoveling motion ate them, never taking his eyes off his brother.

"What *do* you think you're doing?" asked Luther.

"Just greasin' the slide," said Marvin, and addressed the bird, with a greater seriousness than he afforded his brother. Leg, thigh, breast, with the deftness of a surgeon and the inexorable steadiness of a sawmill, Marvin worked away at one hemisphere of the turkey. He did not seem to chew so much as grind the meat. After a half hour or so the company forgot about him. There were other rivalries and side events: who could eat the most sweet potatoes, the most broccoli, the most biscuits with blackberry jam?

Once in a while someone would call to Marvin and offer him some turkey and everyone would laugh. But mostly he was ignored, like Columbus, like the Wright brothers, like any adventurer who appears to have undertaken an exercise in folly. And Marvin labored in the blissful oblivion reserved for visionaries, for all those destined to enlarge the bounds of human experience. One by one the boys abandoned the table, holding their sides, groaning, to sit and stare under the pecan tree in the back yard, roll and doze.

The dishes were cleared away until nothing was left on the table but the monumental Marvin, now balloon-faced, still chewing, very slowly, and his turkey resembling a bombed church, or a Spanish galleon at the bottom of the sea. He seemed to work in a trance, nothing alive but his jaws grinding as he lifted the last morsels of turkey into his full mouth, dropped his fork ringing onto the china and banged his forehead against the table. Out cold.

The turkey carcass gleamed like a museum fossil. The family gathered around the comatose Marvin, whispering and pointing to the wreckage of the turkey. Luther slapped Marvin on the back and he raised up, head lolling like a bear's, eyes rolling. The boys heaved him onto their shoulders and carried him out, green in the face, all around the yard. They set him down in a place of honor under the pecan tree where nature might take its course, and hung the carcass of the ruined turkey on a branch above his head.

My Uncle Orville loved to tell that story. He had been a world-class eater in his boyhood, eating with intense passion and at great length. He had witnessed Marvin's encompassing of the turkey in 1937 and recounted it with conviction, inspiring us to honor that memory while maintaining a sensible humility. We would not make ourselves sick vying with Marvin's legend.

My Uncle Orville loved that story as he loved all of the past. He told the story to Marie and me before dinner, while he was digging. His round face beamed under the visor of the baseball cap he removed to wipe his brow, one foot at rest on the shovel blade. Children scurried around him. Uncle Orville had been digging for days in a camel-shaped mound down the hill where the river hooked into the blue bay.

He was digging for Indians. For years the black loam near the saltmarsh had been turning up arrowheads. My uncle reckoned the camel-shaped mound was a native American landfill, with who knows what pre-Columbian treasures buried within! His shovel had already unearthed some pottery shards, arrowheads and hewn stones that, held up to the light, in good faith resembled tomahawks; and there was a fish bone with a hole bored in one end that must have served some squaw for a sewing needle.

My uncle was digging to work up his appetite for Thanksgiving dinner. Also he was keeping the children from the parlor, where they might overturn the wineglasses, and from the kitchen, where my grandmother was guiding the cuisine toward its grand finale. There is no finer babysitter than a hole in the ground. My uncle had the children to help him dig, and the dog, Grundoon, who was excellently suited to the business. Part retriever, part dachshund, Grundoon was built low but had considerable speed and enthusiasm. He led the party. From a distance the half-blind Grundoon could be seen racing across the horizon toward the camel-shaped Indian mound, and vanish, suddenly, as if he had entered another dimension, when actually he had dropped into the hole. While my uncle paused in his digging to finish the tale of Marvin and the turkey, Grundoon carried on, the black soil and oyster shells flying from beneath him in a steady stream. My grandmother rang the dinner bell, and we climbed the hill to wash up before the feast.

The dining room table had been stretched by inner leaves to three times its normal size to accommodate the crowd, which was backed against the walls and spilled over into the parlor, where children and more distant relatives made do at linen-covered card tables. There was a turkey and a ham at every table. There were billowing clouds of mashed potatoes in china bowls, baskets of golden cornbread and biscuits, steaming under white napkins. There were beets, blood red, and boat-shaped bowls of cranberries the color of rubies.

I was light-headed with hunger, and I was nervous. This year I had been designated to lead the grace before dinner. Looking for the perfect prayer I had read through all the psalms of David, but they seemed so very old-fashioned I decided to make up a new one.

We are gathered after the harvest,
The table is stretched and full
With good wine and meat and bread.
We are glad so many are with us
And pray for the distant and dead.
Should any child feel afraid
Or hurt, let the child call
On kind judges, mothers and fathers,
And each shall receive his own.
For each child has his God in our house
And all of the Gods have their God,
And we are all wealthy beyond reason.

I stood behind my chair to the left of my grandfather as everyone around the table sang:

We gather together to ask the Lord's blessing
He chastens and hastens, His will to
make known . . .

and when the singing was done I took my prayer from my breast pocket and read it loudly, in a quavering voice. In the respectful silence I could feel pride, and perplexity, but most of all the desire to get on with the feasting. A ringing *Amen* filled the house, my grandfather whacked me between the shoulder blades and my Uncle Orville, who so loves the past, said to me, "Sir, you are two thousand years old," a compliment I was too young to appreciate.

I do not know how to tell you about the eating. You have your own stories of mountainous banquets, and folks with appetites like mountaineers who will scale any culinary Everest simply "because it is there." We did not eat like those heroes of the Depression, who had an entire childhood of hunger to prepare them for their miracles of gluttony. We did not eat like Marvin, or Paul Bunyan, or Homer's Cyclops. But we ate proudly, and bravely, and we ate, by the grandfather clock, for a long time. My little cousin David ate half a small turkey, forty-nine spears of asparagus, and one entire mince pie. My Uncle Paul, a lean, wry man, alarmed us by dispatching a baked ham festooned with pineapple slices. My Aunt Jane, with the hollow leg, ate fourteen sweet potatoes, two fat turkey legs, three heads of cauliflower and eleven biscuits. Somebody's baby ate half a bayberry candle. I ate a breast of turkey drowned in gravy, a pound of ham, a hill of mashed potatoes, several dozen brussels sprouts, assorted breads, oyster stuffing, chestnut stuffing and finally a slice each of pumpkin, mince and pecan pie.

After dinner my mother played the piano, and those eccentrics who had eaten moderately sang from the hymnal while those who had upheld tradition went to loll and roll under the pecan tree that had witnessed generations of stunned gluttons.

My Uncle Orville and I were commiserating with each other when the dog, Grundoon, came running with what looked like a stick in his mouth, and the charming look that dogs get when they want to play "fetch." My uncle grabbed for the stick.

It was a bone. It was a *large* bone, with a knob at one end, like the bone in a cartoon, gleaming white where it was not caked with loam. My uncle and I looked at the bone, and then at each other.

"Grundoon!" said my uncle. The dog eyed the bone, ready to run for it as soon as my uncle would let fly. I got up, which was not easy, and followed my uncle down the hill toward the camel-shaped mound beyond which the bay was glowing in the sunset of Indian summer. The crowd followed. The dog was yapping, wild, racing around us, leaping to paw at my uncle's vest. As we neared the crest of the hill where my uncle had opened the Indian mound we saw that Grundoon had been hard at work piling up something of a mound of his own. My uncle was first over the hill, and his jaw dropped as he looked into the hole.

There was an Indian in it. The Indian was sitting up. In a flash I recalled a picture I had seen in a book, the cross-section of an Indian burial mound where they buried their dead in that sitting position, so as to be alert in death when meeting the Great Spirit. The skull and ribs of the Indian were imbedded in the bank of the exposed mound, and the Indian grinned at us, amazed and paternally indulgent. Time had reduced him to essentials. The dog had dislodged a thigh bone, and where the lower half of the skeleton should have been there was a pile of scattered bones. My uncle, with infinite gentleness, placed the missing thigh bone on the pile, waved the rest of us away, and began filling in the Indian mound, under ribbons of cloud turned crimson by the setting sun.

My cousin David was afraid, so my aunt carried him inside to rock him in the ladderback chair next to the stove. Under the pecan tree in the gathering shadows there was a conference to decide what might be done. "Are you sure it's an Indian?" asked Uncle Paul. Uncle Orville assured him that it was. "Perhaps we should call the mayor," said my mother. "Or the archaeologists at the Smithsonian," said my Aunt Jane. "They may want to study the mound."

"No," said my grandmother, who usually had the last word in family matters. "We will leave the Indian in peace."

Back in the parlor there were stories, but no more stories about eating. My uncles told of the idiot brothers, who lived under the bridge subsisting on raw fish and calamus, told stories of the mad physicians of yesteryear who would bury people alive, and one who tried to pull a fishhook from a boy's hand the wrong way. Stories of brute strength and foolishness and blind love and second sight. Some people, secretly, guiltily stole into the pantry to pick at a turkey carcass. My grandfather got out the brandy, and it was time for the children to be in bed.

I lay awake thinking of the Indian. I had a strong sense that something important had been left unsaid, undone. I got into my clothes, crept down the back stairs, out the door and into the warm moonlight of Indian summer. I walked toward the river, where the moon cast a snaky reflection toward the riverbank and the camel-shaped mound. Now the mound looked truly like a fresh grave. Under the grand jury of late November stars I read my Thanksgiving prayer to the buried Indian, feeling that if he could hear it via the Great Spirit, the Indian would understand. And when I had finished that grace I climbed the hill toward my grandmother's house, which shone against the night sky like a good memory.